# Captured by Love

## THE BACHELOR'S CLUB BOOK 2

## Lisa Vanoni

**EABooks Publishing**
Your Partner In Publishing

Cover designer: Robin Black
Cover photo: iStock-Nadtochiy

ISBN: 978-1-963611-45-8

Published by EA Books Publishing, a division of
Living Parables of Central Florida, Inc. a 501c3
EABooksPublishing.com

*To my boys, Andrew, and Michael. Keep trusting in God and you can conquer anything.*

*For God hath not given us the spirit of fear; but of power, and of love and of a sound mind.*

—2 Timothy 1:7 KJV

# Table of Contents

1. Kate . . . . . . . . . . . . . . . . . . . . . . . . . . . . . . . . . . . . . . . . 1

2. The Wedding . . . . . . . . . . . . . . . . . . . . . . . . . . . . . . 15

3. The Basement . . . . . . . . . . . . . . . . . . . . . . . . . . . . . . 23

4. New Information . . . . . . . . . . . . . . . . . . . . . . . . . . . 39

5. The Quiet Kate . . . . . . . . . . . . . . . . . . . . . . . . . . . . . 53

6. The Dance . . . . . . . . . . . . . . . . . . . . . . . . . . . . . . . . . 63

7. Mistletoe . . . . . . . . . . . . . . . . . . . . . . . . . . . . . . . . . 75

8. Too Much . . . . . . . . . . . . . . . . . . . . . . . . . . . . . . . . . 87

9. Love Seeketh Not Her Own . . . . . . . . . . . . . . . . . . . . 99

10. A Beautiful Spring Night . . . . . . . . . . . . . . . . . . . . . 107

11. A New Beginning . . . . . . . . . . . . . . . . . . . . . . . . . . . 121

Discussion Questions . . . . . . . . . . . . . . . . . . . . . . . . . . 125

# CHAPTER 1

# Kate

FRIDAY, SEPTEMBER 19, 1890
BEN'S HOUSE, RAVEN CREST, Idaho

"You're getting married!" Scowling, Jonah leaned back in his chair. *Of course he is. Ben's carried Erin's torch for months now.*

"December first is the date she wants." Benjamin shuffled the cards for the poker game, a silly grin sprawled over his face. "She says it will snow for us, but I keep telling her that's a little early. I waited to tell you all because I proposed again, with the ring and her ma watching. Then she asked if it could just be between us for a bit."

Corbin rolled his eyes and laughed. "Women! How many times do you need to propose? But I think I understand the desire for some privacy. Soon her ma will be telling everyone and planning everything. But, what's the hurry? If she wants snow why not wait. It's always white by January and into February."

"Well . . . " Ben made piles of poker chips, his cheeks reddening to a deep crimson.

*What's he so embarrassed about? Oh, yeah, the honeymoon after the wedding.* Jonah inwardly groaned.

Ben cleared his throat. "It will be about four months by the time December gets here. And we went back and forth for several months before that. We're ready to start our lives together. No more interruptions. Of course, we want Jared to marry us. And Corbin will stand up with me," he looked at Corbin who readily agreed. "But Jonah? Paul? Will you?"

Scratching at his whiskers, Jonah exhaled. "They will be watching you and Erin not me and I don't have to say anything. Aye, I will."

"What about you, Paul?" Ben pushed a stack of chips to each man.

Looking down, Paul took the deck of cards and began dealing with a quick shrug. "Ante up everyone. Five-card draw. No wilds."

Jared tossed in his chips. "So, you're the first one of us to get engaged. Congratulations."

Ben glanced at Paul. "Well, not the first."

Giving a quick shake of his head, Paul silently told everyone he wouldn't talk about his past.

"I'll get that story out of you some day," the Reverend insisted.

"What story? Yeah, I'll stand up with you. Are we gonna play cards or what?" Paul ran his sentences together so fast it sounded like one long word.

They all knew not to pester Paul when he didn't want to talk. Everyone but Jared knew some pieces of the story, but no one knew everything. Someday, Paul would open up and share but today was not that day.

Jonah fanned his cards, and then slapped his forehead. "That explains it."

"Explains what? What are you talking about?" Jared asked.

"Earlier today, at the store, Mrs. Goodwin, Mayor's wife, invited me to a welcome home party for her daughter, Kate. It should be sometime in November, I think." He rolled his head. "Thanks Ben. Now I'm the 'poor bachelor' to set up."

"I almost feel sorry for you," Ben chuckled.

"What happened to keeping it a secret? What does Miss Goodwin's return have to do with Ben and Erin?" Jared looked around confused.

Adding a small stack of chips to the growing pile, Ben explained. "Erin and Kate have been close friends since childhood. Erin sent Kate a wire asking her to come home to be part of the wedding. Word must be spreading already."

Paul tossed in a large pile of chips. "Anyone care to match that?"

Corbin dropped his cards down. "Too rich for my blood."

"I'm out." Jared added his cards to the stack Corbin had started.

Jonah studied Paul carefully. *He thinks he has a good hand but not good enough.* He pushed in a pile of chips. "I'll match that."

Ben conceded, "No good for me. And I will need all your help moving out of here when the time comes."

"So, you're moving into her place?" Corbin teased.

"Legally they're both her places." Ben smiled. "So we're just picking the bigger one."

"I call ya." Jonah leaned forward, looking for the cards.

"A full house. Aces over queens." Paul reached for the stack of chips.

"Not so fast. I have a pair of jacks." Jonah laid his pair down. "And another pair of jacks. That's four of a kind." Jonah playfully pushed Paul's hands out of the way and pulled the stack to himself.

Paul gaped at the hand. "Well, you win this round. But the night is still young."

Corbin shuffled and dealt the next hand.

Wrinkling his brows, Paul wondered out loud. "Hey, Ben, does this mean no more poker nights? How can you be part of The Bachelor's Club if you're married?"

"Erin wants me to keep coming. It will just have to be four bachelors plus one. She says when it's our turn, she'll make a big pot of chili and leave so we can be as disgusting as we want."

Agreeing, each member picked up his cards and inspected them carefully.

Paul tossed his cards face down. "What do people think we do here if we can 'be as disgusting as we want'?"

That was met with shrugs and chuckles.

"Whatcha gonna do with this place?" Jonah inquired, shuffling the deck, and dealing a new hand. He called the game and all eyes focused on the cards in their hands.

Ben glanced at Jared, "Well, we are going to donate it to the church . . . for a parsonage."

Jared's head popped up. "What? A parsonage? But the boarding house . . . and . . . ummm . . ."

"When we leave for Boise, Mrs. Ashburn will move my personal things out and scrub this place down. Then, she will help you move your things in. And stop arguing. It's not for you: it's for the church and for God."

Jared nodded, "I'll try to remember that. And thank you. I'm sure God will return the blessing a hundred fold."

Rolling one shoulder, Ben tossed in his ante, "I'll leave that to God. But everyone else needs to feed the kitty."

The games staggered on until Jared won the night's chips. "Proverbs 18:22," he declared. "Last year Paul picked a verse in 1 Corinthians about not touching a woman. We do need to be careful, but marriage is a gift from God." Jared nudged Ben. "And don't forget it."

"If I do, you can remind me." Ben cleaned up the table. "Edith will get this in the morning when she comes. And this is good timing, she's getting hitched in a few weeks, so she won't be cleaning house for me anymore. Erin insists on doing it herself."

Jonah added the stacks of chips to the poker case. "I gotta get home. Mama has been chomping at the bit all day to tell me something. Now I know what it is." He glanced out the front window. "And it's pouring outside." Pulling his coat tight around him, Jonah yelled out "Night!" He rushed out the door and hurried home.

At the front door, he dreaded going in. *I'm gonna hear everything she knows and then the questions will start about me getting married. Brace yourself. Ben has Erin now, but I like being alone. I need my quiet.*

He pushed the front door open, and Mama didn't disappoint him, a stream of talking and questions flowed. After leaving his wet coat by the fire to dry, Jonah wandered into the kitchen, grabbed some cookies from the jar and poured a glass of milk. He dropped into his chair at the table and dunked a cookie in the milk.

Mama rambled on for several more minutes, eying Jonah as he ate his cookies in silence. Finally, Mama took a deep breath. "All right. I know what that silence means. I have talked too much. Finish your milk and cookies then go to bed. But you know what I am praying for now, don't you?"

Jonah gulped down the last of his milk and kissed Mama goodnight. "You just keep praying. He has a lot to do before I'm ready, if I'm ever ready. Maybe I'll be like St. Paul and stay single. Only God knows." *And God, I'm in no hurry to find out anything different. Batchin' it feels really good.*

MONDAY, NOVEMBER 10
RAVEN CREST IDAHO, THE Goodwins' house
"Jonah Layton? *The undertaker!*" Kate gasped. "Mother!"

Kate anxiously glanced around the dining room. "Where is Father? I need his help."

Father entered the dining room and kissed Mother. "Good evening my darling." He walked around the edge of the table and kissed Kate on the top of her head. "Good evening."

Sitting down, Father tucked a napkin in his collar. "Is that a new dress Kate? That's a pretty blue. It makes your eyes sparkle."

"Thank you. I bought it in Paris just before coming home." She puffed the sleeves just a little. "And it is cobalt not blue." She smiled warmly to Father, "You always could charm the spots off a cow. But I need your help and right now."

He looked closer at Kate. "Did you do something to your hair? It looks darker? Almost black."

"No Father, my hair has just darkened as I have matured. No need to worry. I do not color it like some women are starting to do. But I do need your help. Mother wants to invite Jonah Layton, *the undertaker*, to the welcome home party."

Mother rang the small bell next to her. "Dinner will be served momentarily. Leonard, Kate has been home almost a week, and you are just now noticing her darker hair?" Mother gave Father a slight, rueful glare. Turning her attention back to Kate, she directed the conversation back to the welcome home party. "And about the guest list, of course Erin and Benjamin will be at the party. I have also included Pastor Morris. I just thought it would be nice to invite Mr. Layton also. Our town has grown since you left several years ago. It is polite to invite notable members of Raven Crest to this party. It looks like it will be next Saturday evening."

"I understand Mother. But he is an *undertaker*. That vocation is so . . . " Kate rolled her shoulders and grimaced, trying to express her distaste.

"If you want Pastor Morris to join us, you will have to have it on another night. He has standing plans on Saturdays." Father suggested.

"And what plans does he have on Saturdays? I know he is part of The Bachelor's Club, but they meet on Friday nights." Mother dished a slice of roast beef onto her plate.

Father shook his head, refusing to give further information. "It doesn't matter. Maybe a buffet instead of a sit down dinner would be best. And Kate, Jonah does important work in our community. He's not *just* the undertaker but that by itself is important."

Kate sighed a deep, frustrated sigh. "I suppose it's up to you Mother. I don't really know the man."

Her mother smiled. "Good, because I have already invited him. I saw him at the store several weeks ago and before I knew it, the invitation slipped out." Then with a quizzical look, she pondered, "Sometimes I think he throws away written invitations."

Father chuckled. "He does avoid social engagements when he can."

Kate inhaled and exhaled quickly trying to regain her composure before she became upset. *Find something good in this. She was not trying to take over.* "Thank you Mother for thinking ahead. The social gatherings here are different than European society. I know I will need some time to readjust to Raven Crest."

Absentmindedly, Kate rubbed her thumb over the glass in front of her. "Everything has been so well planned for me up until now. After school here, I went to school in New York. Then I was off to Europe with friends. My time was full of travel and parties. Now, I am back here for Erin's wedding, but after that I am unsure of how to spend my time. Raven Crest is so different than what I was used to in Europe."

"I understand, and I will help. Maybe you can assist in the winter dance planning. That might get your sights back in Raven Crest. Our Thanksgiving dinner needs finishing touches, too."

"It is a start, I suppose." Kate poked at her meat. "Some fish would be nice. I didn't get fresh-caught fish in Europe. They had good recipes, but it wasn't the same."

"I might be able to solve that problem." Father sliced his meat and took a sip of wine.

"You are not going ice fishing, Leonard Goodwin. Get that through your thick skull right now. Maybe the butcher has some fish, but you will stay off that ice. Do you understand?" Mother brandished her fork with a warning glare.

Father conceded. "Yes dear. Maybe I can get some young buck to catch a few for us. And besides, the waters aren't frozen yet. Icy, but not frozen."

After Kate finished the meal, she dabbed her mouth with a napkin. "The dinner was wonderful Mother. Shall we go in the parlor and look at what is planned so far for the winter dance?"

"Yes, of course. I have the planning book at the desk already."

Following her mother into the parlor, Kate glimpsed her reflection in the mirror. *My hair is darker. It's almost as black as Mother's hair, without the sprinkles of gray, of course.*

Father reclined on the sofa and began to read the evening paper. Kate looked over the notes Mother offered. *Santa? Toys? I thought this was a dance.*

Kate scratched some questions in the notebook. Who is playing the music? Are the hors d'oeuvres catered or voluntary? Who is organizing them?

"Hors d'oeuvres?" Mother read the notes over Kate's shoulder. "Oh my, Kate, it has been a while since you have been here. We serve cookies and some other finger treats. The women from the town bring them. You must tell me more about the parties you attended."

"Mmmm. The galas were scrumptious. Wonderful orchestras, and such delights. But something seemed to be missing. I think it was the homey touch of everyone involved. Sometimes I felt like a fish out of water."

Mother settled on a wingback chair nearby. "How so?"

"Well, I just used the phrase 'a fish out of water' and you knew what I meant. So part of me is still that small hometown girl. But after school and travels, I wondered if I could ever come back here and feel comfortable again. I have to learn how to be a woman in a small town, not a small-town girl. I will figure it out. Erin seems to have adjusted well."

"Yes, she has." Father glanced over his paper. "But she had some challenges also. She began by helping Miss Burns. Then, she had an uphill battle with learning how to be a woman in a man's business world. She is still learning many things with the help of her father and Ben."

Kate giggled. "I barely remember Mr. Hammond. By the time I was interested in boys, he was out of school and off to college."

"Now you will have a whole team of people ready to make your acquaintance. That is, eligible, young men ready to grab the eye of a beautiful young lady." Father praised.

"Father . . ." Kate smiled demurely, and playfully swatted at her father. "Mother, shall we continue?"

Later that night, Kate sat on her bed with her Bible open, thinking of the undertaker. "God, am I doing it again?"

Kate had grown up in church but hadn't taken it seriously. Then, one day, in Europe, she visited the Sistine Chapel. Her friends marveled over the artwork on the ceiling, but Kate was caught up in the stories. God created *her* and loved *her;* Christ had died for *her.*

After leaving the chapel, Kate returned to her room. She prayed the prayer she had heard so many times. Kate confessed her sins, accepted Christ's sacrifice, and invited Him to be Lord of her life.

While visiting different countries and towns, Kate tried to find churches to attend, and her friends poked fun a little. But they were more concerned about her being around "the right" people.

Kate found herself judging people based on their stations in life, just as her friends did. Then she began to ask God to help her see people through His eyes, not hers. When she heard from Erin, she came home, leaving her friends and hoping for a new start.

Deep in her heart, Kate knew she was judging Mr. Layton by his profession not through God's eyes. *Show me, Lord. I want to please You,* she prayed silently.

Flipping through her Bible, Kate hoped to find some relief from her nagging conscience. Instead, she found the second chapter of James, a passage about treating the rich and the poor the same.

"All right God," she whispered in an exasperated tone. "I'll *try* to include him. But his job gives me the willies." She added a shiver, just to make her point.

SATURDAY, NOVEMBER 22

Jonah rode his horse, Pepper, to the Goodwins' house with a plan of escape in mind. The street in front of the house was littered with buggies and horses, hinting of the crowd inside. Jonah could already feel the people surrounding him.

*I will stay for one hour. It helps if I know how long I will be here. I need to find a wall to stand by and hope no one notices me.* He stroked his beard. *Most of the pox scars have been covered for years. No one will see them. And just forget what happened when you were a boy. This isn't school. That lisp is gone now.*

Ben and Erin arrived in Ben's buggy with the new team he had just bought, Liberty and Bell. Mama had chosen his team's names, Salt and Pepper. He had wanted Heaven and Hades, but Mama reminded him not everyone enjoys such dark humor. Some may take offense, she said, so she insisted on simpler and safer names.

Ben patted Jonah on the back as he and Erin entered the room. "Deep breath. Where's your ma?"

"Still with Esther in Boise. I'm alone tonight."

"Oh, of course, that's where you were for Thanksgiving. Well, if you need me, I'm here. You can do this."

Jonah forced a shaky smile and found a corner to lean into. Ben and Erin walked around, laughing, and making small talk. Jared was there, honoring his weekly fast by refusing the refreshments and he was having no trouble mingling with the large group too.

*How can they hobnob so easily?* Jonah wondered.

Memories soared though his mind of being a young boy in school, of the headmaster making him stand in front of the class with his smallpox scars and lisp, to recite imperfect lessons.

*I can do this. With God's help, I can do this. He will never leave me or forsake me.*

Jonah smiled politely to the hired help carrying trays of small delights. He shook his head at the man offering champaign glasses. But gratefully, no one noticed him standing alone in a corner, that is, until Mayor Goodwin maneuvered over to Jonah.

Jonah smiled weakly. *Someone noticed me. But it is Mayor. I can talk with him a little. And my hour is almost up.*

"Thanks for coming. I know you hate these things." Mayor Goodwin parked in front of Jonah blocking his escape route.

Jonah shrugged, unsure of how to respond politely.

"I have a favor to ask of you."

Now Jonah was intrigued. People seldom asked for his help considering his vocation.

"My daughter, Kate," he inclined his chin toward a young woman in a deep blue and white dress. "She needs . . . some . . . uh . . . lessons in real life."

Jonah wrinkled his brow unsure of Mayor's meaning.

Mr. Goodwin laughed "Nothing so serious. I noticed she tends to ride a high horse." He shrugged, "She looks down on others sometimes. Perhaps, after the wedding is over, could she come to visit you a few times so she can see all you do? I know you do more than the undertaker position. I thought helping with the toys might get her to see how fortunate she is."

Closing his eyes for a second, Jonah inhaled deeply. "Yes, she can come over."

"Thank you. She needs to understand there is more to life than parties. Seeing the other job you do might help too. But not too soon . . . after all, she is my baby . . . Maybe, if that service is needed . . . I don't know what I'm saying any more." Mayor Goodwin chuckled.

Jonah half grinned. "It's all right, I know what you mean. But now, I will be going home."

He sidestepped Mayor Goodwin, said goodbye to Mrs. Goodwin, and made eye contact with Ben, letting Ben know he was leaving. He hopped on Pepper and headed for home. Jonah needed his basement and the quiet solitude he found there.

*Thank You Lord, for helping me through that hour. Now I need to figure out what I will do when Miss Goodwin shows up. I would have to talk to her and entertain her. I don't know how to do that. A woman alone is just as nerve wracking as a crowd of people. I need Your help.*

SUNDAY, NOVEMBER 23
RAVEN CREST RIVER

Jonah cast his line into the river. A few small slabs of ice floated by as he slowly paced the bank. He gave his line a quick wiggle. No bite. Soon he decided to recast back up stream. Ben silently reeled his line in and met Jonah upstream ready to recast his line.

*This can't get better. Fishing with a good friend, who is content with being quiet.*

Jonah felt the telltale tug of his line. He pulled it in just a bit, letting the fish take a good bite. The bobber sank. "Yes! That feels like a big one."

"Well, let's see." Ben pulled his line in and re-baited the hook.

"Sure is a good one. Just need about two or three more." Jonah remarked.

"Three? Is Esther and her family coming over?"

"Naw. I got enough here for several good fillets for Mama and me. But Mr. Goodwin was taking an after church stroll with his wife when he saw me packing up. Mrs. Goodwin has laid down the law about fishing when the water is icy. So, he asked for a few. I suppose three. One for each of them."

BANG!

Gunfire echoed in the small forest nearby. Jonah winced and stiffened.

Ben pulled in his line. "Here, I got enough, you can have one of mine. Nanna says she'll teach Erin how to cook trout no matter what. Erin has made one attempt so far but wouldn't let me try it." He released the fish into Jonah's bucket. "You all right? I think that was Corbin."

Jonah nodded slowly, staring at the icy water. "I'll be fine. You used to hunt with your pa. Why don't you hunt anymore?"

"I go on occasion with Corbin, but I only get enough for what I need and that is it. Corbin really enjoys it. Sleeping under the stars, cooking over a campfire, and eating outside. He hunts a lot.

I think he sells most of it to the butcher for some extra income. I can do it. I just don't enjoy it like he does."

Ben tossed another fish into Jonah's bucket. "I think you have enough. Are you gonna clean them before taking them to the Goodwins'?"

Jonah glanced at the bucket. "Aye. I will clean all of them. Mama won't be home 'till tomorrow. I'll fillet them and put ours in the ice box."

"I'll help. Last time I was cleaning fish for someone else, it was Miss Burns." A sad, reminiscent smile slowly formed across Ben's face.

Silently, the men began cleaning and filleting the fish.

"I used to do this with my papa. Still hurts sometimes." Jonah mumbled.

Ben nodded. "I feel the same way sometimes. Pa taught me to fish and clean them too."

"But you got Erin now."

"Yes I do, and I need to take these to the Ashburn's." Ben carried his bucket of fillets on one arm and fishing gear on the other.

Jonah finished the last fish and shouldered his gear. The walk home was quiet and peaceful. A few couples strolled around town enjoying the nippy autumn air, but Jonah was left alone, the way he liked it.

He set the bucket on the kitchen counter and added a few fillets to the icebox, then he warmed his hands over the small fire burning in the cook stove. Jonah rotated his hands back and forth accepting the slight sting on his numb fingers until a pleasant warmth spread up his arms. He opened his coat, inviting the heat in.

*Now to the Goodwin house. Take Salt. She likes the rides better than Pepper. I need to give them both a good rub down when I get back. Too bad Mama's not here. I could use her as an excuse to get home if someone were to talk to me.*

Jonah chuckled as he saddled Salt. *Papa told her not to step in too much when I was a child. I think she blames herself a little for me being so bashful.* He straddled Salt and rode to the Goodwin house, the bucket of fish tapping softly near his leg. *I'll leave these at the back door. I think the Goodwins' have a cook, but she may not be there; after all it is Sunday. Or does she live there?*

Another horse and rider met him at the corner of the Goodwins' street. A woman with dark hair, wearing a royal blue riding habit, sat primly on her horse, and trotted up beside him.

"What a beautiful day for a ride. Mother and Father wanted their walk. But on days like this I need the fresh country air." She breathed deeply filling her lungs.

*Is that Miss Goodwin? No one around here wears such fine riding clothes. That blue riding dress is the darkest I've ever seen. Jumpin' Jehosaphat! Those blue eyes sparkle!*

Jonah tried to clear his head. "Ummm, Miss Goodwin?"

"Oh yes, and you are?"

"Jonah Layton." The words seemed to stick in his throat. He held out the bucket. "Fish . . . your pa . . ."

Miss Goodwin stopped her horse in front of the house and smiled brightly. "You must come in and show Father what you've caught for him. I admit that I am the one that asked for fish one night at dinner."

Jonah shook his head. "Can't . . . ummm, Mama waiting . . . home . . . Bye" He thrust the bucket into her hands and hurried Salt home. *Mama's not home. Didn't mean to lie; just got flustered, is all.*

At home, he dismounted Salt and walked her into the stable. Jonah gave her a good brush down and cleaned her hooves. He walked around Salt and patted her nose. "Girl, you're the only one I can talk too." He nuzzled Salt a little, then his head popped up. "Oh no! She's the one. She's the one Mr. Goodwin wants to come help me." He rested his forehead on Salt's nose. "What am I gonna do? She's not just a strange woman, but she's pretty and likes to talk. Oh, Lord, help me, please."

CHAPTER 2

# The Wedding

The five bachelors, soon to be four bachelors plus one, met in Jared's office at the church. Ben paced the floor nervously. His friends lightly joked at Ben and his jitters.

"So Erin got her wish. It's snowing just a little outside. But you look like a long-tailed cat in a room full of rockers." Corbin guffawed.

Jonah stretched his legs under Jared's desk. "I got my wish, a good pork dinner. I heard there will be rice too. I'm happy."

Ben glared a friendly, nervous stare at his friends. He sucked in a deep, playful warning breath and growled out an exhale. Silently he prayed, *Lord, am I ready for this? Can I do everything I'm about to promise? She deserves so much better than me, but she tells me that I deserve better than her. Help me to be the man You want me to be.*

Checking his pocket watch, Jared gathered the men around Ben. "We need to pray before we go out there."

Together, the four groomsmen prayed over Ben and the new marriage.

Ben inhaled deeply and announced, "At the reception, Erin wants the wedding party to dance one dance together. Let's go." He opened the door and walked to the front of the church before anyone could argue. Behind him were mumblings and whispered complaints, but Ben knew his friends would not let him down.

Stationed near the pulpit with his friends next to him, Ben carefully, anxiously watched the church doors, knowing that Erin would soon come through them.

The front doors slowly swung open revealing the bridesmaids. But Ben's gaze rested on the sight behind them . . . Erin.

She wore a flowing white dress. One arm held a Bible close to her; the other arm was wrapped in her father's arm.

Her father, Judge Ashburn mouthed some words. Ben was sure the judge said to Erin, "I love you."

Erin's chin moved but the veil covering her face hid her too well for Ben to tell what she said. She must have returned her father's sentiment.

For one moment Ben's heart ached. He missed his parents more than words could explain. *Thank You, God, that Erin has her parents to share this day with her.*

Tears welled in his eyes as she slowly walked down the aisle toward him.

*And thank You, Lord, for this beautiful woman.*

Jonah shifted, trying to discreetly hide behind Corbin and Ben. Paul stood behind him and softly kicked his heel, telling him to be still. But too many people were looking at him. Fighting the urge to run away, he reminded himself, *"They're not watching me; they are watching Ben.*

The church door opened, and Kate Goodwin led the ladies out.

*She's the one coming to my house. How could anyone have such thick, dark curls? How does she get them piled on her head so perfectly? Does she know how pretty she is? That is such a soft blue, Erin must have picked it out; all the ladies are wearing it. But it's beautiful on her; it makes her eyes sparkle. I need to look at something else . . . anything but her.*

Ben cleared his throat, finally grabbing Jonah's attention away from Miss Goodwin. Through the reflection in the large glass window, Jonah noticed the tears sparkling in Ben's eyes and the nervous anticipation on his face. Another emotion seemed to be there too.

*Delight? Must be love.* Jonah's heart warmed, wondering if someday he would have the same expression on his face.

Occasionally, Jonah cast a glance at Kate. Some vague images of a talkative little girl filtered through his mind, but he could recall no clear memories. He forced his attention back to Jared and the ceremony in process. Now was not the time to let his thoughts wander.

After the vows, Jared said, "You may kiss the bride."

Ben gulped as he lifted the veil to kiss Erin. Tears glistened lightly in her eyes. Jonah smiled, trying to control a chuckle. *Mama cries at weddings too. Why do women do that?*

Motioning for the couple to turn around, Jared asked the guests, "May I introduce to you, Mr. and Mrs. Benjamin Hammond?"

The guests cheered. Ben marched Erin down the aisle. Corbin was the first man in line, and he offered his elbow to Miss Goodwin. Jonah smiled weakly at the young blonde woman, batting her eyes, openly flirting with him. He held out his elbow trying to keep as much distance as he could while they promenaded to the town hall. Jonah tried not to wrinkle his nose, but the heavy perfume drifting from the young lady was sickeningly sweet.

The town hall was full of tables surrounding a dance floor. In one corner, a band softly played. The wedding party had a table up front, and a large cake was in another corner.

Jonah took his seat, ready to spend the rest of the evening sitting at his place, eating a delicious meal, and letting all the other guests have their fun.

"Now we need the picture." A short man with a bar handled mustache, directed the bride and groom to the camera.

Erin sat on a chair near the wedding party. "I don't know anyone in Raven Crest that has a wedding photograph," she said.

Ben rested his hand on the back of the chair. "We will be the first then."

"No smiling. Keep a straight face. If you budge the photograph will blur. If you smile you will look undignified." The photographer ducked under a black cloth. "Ready?" *Flash!* A bright light burst. "Hold it. Hold it. There. You are done. The photograph will be ready in a few weeks."

Ben led Erin to the front table. "The happiest day of our lives and it looks like the horses were just stolen."

"But we will have a photograph to always remind us of this day. And remember, we look dignified with straight faces. Did you tell The Club my request?"

"Just as we were walking out of Jared's office. They were taken back but they had no time to argue. They will do it." Ben led Erin back to the table, "I need a quick swallow. Then we can have our first dance. Our first dance as husband and wife." Ben gulped down some water. "Are you ready Mrs. Hammond?"

She took his hand. "I love the sound of that —Mrs. Hammond."

The couple glided around the dance floor and Jonah's knee bounced briskly. *Help me Lord, I forgot about that. She wants us to dance with the bridesmaids. Mama and Esther are the only women I have ever danced with. Now what?*

The band struck a new song. Ben nodded to his friends.

Paul snagged Miss Mary Ashburn's hand; she was Erin's cousin and engaged to a fellow back in Philadelphia, making her a safe dance partner. That left Miss Jenkins and Miss Goodwin.

Jonah's stomach turned. Miss Jenkins was Erin's cousin who had flirted outrageously with him on the way to the hall. And Miss Goodwin was—well—she was Miss Goodwin. Jonah wasn't sure which one would be the hardest to dance with—a flirt or the prettiest woman around.

Corbin gruffly whispered, "You owe me." Forcing a smile, he took Miss Jenkin's hand.

That left Miss Goodwin. Jonah gulped, his palms dampened, and his hands began to shake. *She won't laugh. She is more polite than that, I hope.* Jonah held his hand out to Kate Goodwin.

She daintily rested the tips of her fingers on his open palm, allowing Jonah to lead her to the dance floor. Jonah placed a hand on her back, slightly above her waist and held her other hand. A sweet scent of perfume filled the air.

*That perfume smells nice. Better than that other girl.*

Hands trembling, he led Kate in the waltz. He forced a smile and stared over her shoulder, trying to concentrate on the music and steps. One step was too big, and he landed on his own foot. Jonah clenched his jaws and drew his shoulders up to his ears. He glanced at Kate hoping she didn't notice.

Her bright blue eyes sparkled, and a gentle smile graced her red lips. Jonah was lost in the warmth of it all.

A knot tightened in his belly, encouraging another stumble. Embarrassed, Jonah looked away. *What does she think of me now? And how does she get her lips so red? What did Esther call it . . . lipstick?*

The music ended with claps and cheers from the guests. Ben invited the onlookers to join them for more dancing. Jonah stiffened and dragged Kate back to her seat, grateful to escape the odd sensations engulfing him. He dropped into his chair, glaring at the table. A waiter slid a plate of delicious-looking food in front of him.

*Just enjoy the meal,* he commanded himself. *I don't need to think about anything else right now. Just eat.*

Jonah picked up his fork, then dropped it at the sight of Jared standing up, remembering they needed to pray. Jared asked God to blessed the meal, the new couple and those involved with the reception.

The pork and rice seemed to make everything right with the world again. After clearing his plate, Jonah leaned back in his chair, watching Ben and Erin glide around the dance floor, lost in each other's arms.

Mayor Goodwin strolled over to Jonah's table. "So, you have met Kate. She will need something to do tomorrow, I'm sure. Can she come visit you like we discussed?"

Jonah's knee began to bob again. "She can come over. I don't know what she will do, but I guess that can be figured out tomorrow."

"Wonderful. And much obliged for your help." Mayor held out his hand, offering a friendly shake. Jonah accepted, then turned his attention to the empty plate.

After Mayor Goodwin left, Jonah began to silently grumble. *How did I get myself into this? Maybe Mama won't let her in the basement. It could look improper for a single man and woman to be alone like that, even with Mama there. Maybe Miss Goodwin could help Mama upstairs instead. Maybe—*Mrs. Ashburn interrupted his thoughts.

"It is time for the cake and punch," Mrs. Ashburn announced, shooing Ben and Erin to the corner with an extravagantly frosted three-tiered cake. She gently pulled the top tier off and set it to one side. In front of Ben and Erin was placed the middle tier ready to be cut. Then, she handed them a knife with lots of ribbon attached. "Now, Benjamin, be a gentleman," Mrs. Ashburn playfully warned.

Together, they held the knife and cut the first slice. The crowd applauded. Another slice was cut. Erin put the piece on a plate and smiled demurely at Ben.

Ben was a gentleman and carefully fed Erin the piece of cake. He got a bit of icing on the tip of his finger and playfully wiped it on her nose. It was enough to make Erin laugh but not enough to ruin her dress or hair.

Later, back at the table, Ben elbowed Jonah. He nodded and smiled at Ben. *Erin doesn't suspect a thing. Ben planned this surprise well. After this, I get to go home. Mama already has a ride, so I don't have to take her home. No coming back. No more people. And no more noise, just quiet and home.*

Erin was stunned to hear the clock strike nine. This day had been perfect. *Jonah just left. He must need his quiet. But I can't think about that. Right now I feel like a princess, and Ben is my knight in shining armor.*

Ben leaned over and whispered in her ear, "Are you ready?"

A wealth of emotions washed over her. It was time to leave and go to their house. They would spend the night in Raven Crest and tomorrow, board a train to Boise. But there was still tonight.

Erin nodded with a small tremble. Did Ben feel the same as she? Nervous didn't sum up her many feelings. There were too many to name.

She took his hand and carried her dress train on her other arm as they left the hall. Claps and whistles followed them.

Ben held the door open, and Erin gasped in awe. Jonah sat on top of a white carriage with his team, Salt and Pepper, ready to go.

Looking down from the coachman's seat, Jonah gave a nod of acknowledgment, saying, "Mrs. Hammond."

Erin suppressed a giggle. *Mrs. Hammond. Will I ever get tired of that?*

Ben opened the carriage door and helped her in.

It was only a few blocks to the house, but the princess feeling refused to leave.

At the house, Ben carried her over the threshold, and up the stairs to their bedroom. He kissed her gently, whispering softly in her ear, "I love you, Mrs. Hammond."

# CHAPTER 3

# The Basement

TUESDAY, DECEMBER 2

The morning after the wedding, Kate moped at the breakfast table. Erin was gone on her honeymoon. Mary Ashburn was leaving today for Philadelphia and Emma Jenkins was spending a few days with her family before she left for school.

*She's here a few more days then off to finishing school—because she needs a lot of finishing, Kate thought wryly. Now what will I do? Once Erin comes back, she will be busy with her husband and family. Well, it will take a while for the family, at least nine months.*

Mother patted Kate's hand. "You look like a storm is brewing. Problem?"

"I don't know what to do with myself. Erin is gone for a week. The winter dance planning starts tomorrow. It would be nice if someone needed my help."

Father trotted downstairs. "I'm hungry. And breakfast smells wonderful." He tucked a napkin under his chin. "Oh, and Kate, it's nice to hear you want to help someone. Jonah Layton needs some assistance, so I volunteered you. Make sure to tell him thank you for the fish."

"He's the one who brought the fish?" Kate clarified. Images of the bearded man, stumbling over his words and pushing the bucket of fish to her flew through her mind. He was also the one she had danced with at the wedding. More uncertainty filled her.

"He reminds me of a turtle," Mother commented.

"A turtle? Why?" Kate blew on her hot tea.

Mother softly laughed. "He is simple, like a turtle—slow and deliberate. And he hides in his shell whenever he can."

The long beard and tattered leather hat stuck in her mind's eye. *That must be the definition of ruggedly handsome, but he is almost boyish; he's so shy and awkward.* Kate shook her head quickly. *I've always been attracted to clean-shaven, sophisticated men.*

She began to think about her escorts in Europe. Had she really been attracted to them? The descriptions "stuffy" and "arrogant" came to mind. But with Jonah something was different; something was intriguing.

"When do we leave, Father?" Kate asked, reluctantly trying to get her mind somewhere else.

"Let's eat first. I've got a busy day," Father said, bowing his head in prayer.

Jonah pushed the last bite of pancakes around his plate, dreading the end of breakfast and the beginning of a day of entertaining Miss Goodwin. Mama was boiling water for washing and babbling about yesterday's wedding, oblivious to his dilemma.

"Miss Goodwin's coming over today," Jonah interrupted.

Mama looked at him surprised. "Oh, really?"

Jonah rolled his eyes. "Don't get any ideas. Mayor Goodwin asked if she could come see what I do." He gave his mother an exaggerated helpless look. "Could you take her off my hands?"

Mama smiled and patted his cheek. "You know the answer to that question."

"Would it look improper for us to be alone in the basement?" He asked hopefully.

"No, we are not as staunch as the high society back east. So, as long as the door is open and I am home, it will be fine. Good try, though."

That was met with a head and eye roll, accompanied by an exaggerated moan. Jonah knew Mama wouldn't help but it didn't hurt to ask. Her normal responses were "It's for your own good" or "You got yourself into it; you can get yourself out."

"You used to help, when I was a lad recovering from a deadly disease." He frowned as pathetically as he could, tapping a smallpox scar near his eye.

"Yes, I did. And your papa warned me that I was creating more trouble than I was solving. He told me you would have a challenging time with these things if I kept stepping in. And he was right. So, you are now learning how to be more sociable, whether you like it or not."

Jonah tossed his napkin on his plate. "I'll be downstairs. By myself. At least for a bit. Maybe the ghosts will understand better."

Mama swatted his rump with a kitchen towel. "Don't tease like that. It's disrespectful to the deceased." Folding her arms with a playful glare, Mama joked back, "Besides, the ghosts agree with me—not you."

Jonah belly laughed and jogged down the stairs. In the basement, he could work, pray, and not think about other people or the trouble he'd had as a boy.

A knock on the front door told him it was over, and he would have company soon. Mama's voice drifted down the stairs, informing the mayor and Miss Goodwin where he was.

Jonah looked around in a feeble attempt to find a hiding place. He only found the toys he was working on and the double-wide closet.

His dark humor began to beckon ideas. He imagined himself lying on the floor in the closet with his hands over his chest as if he were dead and the reaction he would get from everyone. He choked down a chuckle and gave up on hiding.

Instead, he picked up a wooden soldier and began the detailed whittling. Miss Goodwin and Mr. Goodwin came to the basement door. Mayor popped his head in just long enough to say, "Thank you for the fish and—" he nodded to Kate and then left.

Scanning the basement, Kate looked as uncomfortable as Jonah felt. She slowly descended the stairs, tossing a glance at the door behind her.

Silently, Jonah directed his attention to a chair and table in the corner. She was just as pretty as he remembered. How could anyone be that pretty?

Kate sat down and fingered the book on the table. She picked it up and began to look through it.

Jonah stifled a grin. He knew what was in the book. It was full of coffin sketches, blanket patterns, and drawings of pillows or other things that a mourner might put in a coffin.

Kate set the book back down with a small shudder, and nervously glanced around the room.

Jonah turned his attention back to his work. He held up the toy soldier, blowing off the dust and scraps.

"What's that?" Kate asked.

*Protection in the afterlife.* His macabre humor bubbled up. However, he choked out a flat reply, "Toy soldier."

Kate's uneasiness was apparent. She looked around the room and her gaze often landed on the door at the top of the stairs. It was open, allowing anyone access in and out of the room.

Eventually, Kate stood and began walking around. She rubbed her shoulders trying to warm them in the frosty basement. The soft snow that had fallen the day before had turned cold and harsh overnight, creating a freeze and the need for a fire in the fireplace. However, Jonah intentionally kept the basement as cold as possible.

She stopped at the pile of toys in one corner. "What are these for?"

Jonah eyed her skeptically, forcing an explanation. "My cousin plays Santa. I help with the toys." *That lisp is gone. No one has heard it in years.*

Kate's eyes traveled from the pile of toys to him, looking at him doubtfully. With a sigh, she knelt on the floor and began to sort the toys. Jonah was hesitant to let her touch them but kept quiet, allowing her to work.

She made one pile of soldiers, another of toy animals and another of boats. He was impressed. Now he could see what he had made and what still needed to be done. Jonah went back to the task at hand and let Kate continue organizing.

*She's not talking like she did at her house. She's quiet, and she helps.* He glanced at her again, sorting the toys. *She's pretty, too. But the helping and quiet are more important.*

Noon came sooner than Jonah expected. The warm kitchen and hot soup would be a welcomed treat from the cold basement.

In the kitchen, Mama and Kate made small talk as they ate. Jonah sat quietly, eating his lunch, watching the two women through his lowered brows.

He caught Mama tactfully pointing to a spot on her chin. He knew this signal; it meant he had food in his beard. He slightly turned in his chair and wiped his whiskers, watching Mama from the corner of his eye. She gave a small nod, informing him the area was cleaned off. He shifted back to face the table, head low and his attention directed at his lunch, trying to keep the long bristles tucked away from his plate.

Although his beard could create problems sometimes, Jonah loved his whiskers. They helped cover the smallpox scars, and it was a fond memory of his father who had also sported a long beard and mustache. Papa had passed ten years earlier in a hunting accident, so the beard and mustache were fond reminders of times with his father teaching him how to care for the set.

Clearing his throat, Jonah muttered, "Going back down. Thanks, Mama."

Kate followed Jonah into the basement. She went to a pile of wood in another corner and began to separate the blocks and planks.

Jonah caught her shivering as she worked. To keep warm, he wore a sweater and work gloves while he was down here, but Miss Goodwin looked cold. She was sitting on the floor and wore a dress with long sleeves, but no gloves or coat.

*Her coat is at the door; no wonder she's shivering. Mama should have something to help her stay warm. No one should be that cold.* He silently went upstairs and brought down a pillow for her to sit on and a blanket to wrap around her shoulders as she worked.

Kate smiled her appreciation and continued.

Jonah finished another toy soldier. Placing it near him on the floor, he caught Kate glaring at him and the toy.

Giving a half grin, he took it to the pile of toy soldiers and examined the order of things. All the toys that had been painted were on one side of the room and the ones that still needed paint were on the other. Now he could easily tell which ones needed paint and which ones were finished. There were some that he had started to paint, but hadn't completed yet, advertising his procrastination.

A knock at the door told them that Mayor Goodwin was here to pick up Kate. She dashed upstairs as properly and quickly as she could. Jonah followed, knowing he would be required to politely say good night and thank you.

Mayor Goodwin asked Jonah tentatively, "Tomorrow?"

"Oh, I have plans tomorrow and Thursday, with the Ladies Auxiliary. We are planning the winter dance," Kate reminded her father.

"Friday then?" He looked from one to the other. Jonah nodded his agreement, and Kate gave a small smile in return.

Gulping, Jonah forced out a mumbled, "Thank you, Miss Goodwin."

The mayor tipped his hat and ushered Kate outside.

Jonah peeked out the window, wondering if there was more to Kate than parties and dresses. *There must be more. I think she's been underestimated. Everyone expects "Kate, the pretty girl that doesn't think much and talks a lot," but deep down there's more, I'm sure.*

"I need to stoke the fire." Jonah turned away from the window toward the fireplace.

Mama stood behind him with a smug grin. "Looks like you survived," she quipped.

"What's for dinner?" Jonah asked, ignoring his mother's comment, and closing the door to anymore conversations about Kate.

Mama exhaled a small laugh. "I do believe I see a blush. And we are having pork chops."

FRIDAY, DECEMBER 5
THE GOODWIN HOUSE

Kate aimlessly stirred butter and sugar into a bowl of oatmeal. *The winter dance committee was fun. It was nice to have something to do for a while, but was that it? It will be next week before they meet again. I guess I will go back to the Layton house, but that basement is odd.* Kate tilted her head in thought. *Is the basement odd or Mr. Layton? Did Mother just ask me something?*

"So, have you noticed all the changes since you left? We used to just have the dance, maybe some cookies and punch. Now we have the Santa giveaway and lots of different desserts, but your help was wonderful. It was just the touch we needed to give some new life to the celebration. Next week, we should start planning the decorations. I'm sure you have many ideas after all the European Christmases."

Her father interrupted with a one-word question. "Jonah's?"

"I suppose it's not as bad as I thought. Yes, I will go again today. But I'm not sure after that," she answered honestly.

"Do you know what I mean when I said he is like a turtle?" Mother asked.

Kate tapped her chin. "He is bashful but there seems to be more. He is—well—odd but in a kind way. The men in Europe were so—dashing. They were polite and suave. If they had any whiskers, it was usually a waxed mustache. But Mr. Layton is different. He is quiet and those long whiskers are interesting. I wonder why he has them."

"They cover his smallpox scars. His father used to have the same set of whiskers." Father gruffly cleared his throat and left the table.

Kate followed. Pinning a beret on, she spun around. "How do I look? I think I will be warm enough."

Father shoved an arm in his coat. "Green? Usually you wear some shade of blue. And I think you are beautiful."

"Thank you, Father. I chose green just for something different. But I feel as wide as a whale; I have so many layers on. That basement is freezing. No heat at all."

As they drove through town, Kate watched boys throwing snowballs at each other on their way to school. Girls walked close together, laughing, and talking. She felt a tender ache for such simpler days. When would life be that easy again?

They arrived at the Layton house, and her father stopped long enough to let her out. She walked up the steps and knocked, unsure.

Jonah answered immediately, settling his hat to leave.

He jutted his chin toward the street, beard whipping in the frigid breeze. "Paintin' today," was his only explanation.

Kate wasn't sure if she was supposed to follow him or not. She pulled her coat a little closer and began to walk with him.

*The worst he could do is tell me to go back to his house,* she assured herself.

The mercantile was a warm relief from the crisp morning gusts. Mr. Thompson had a fire burning in the potbelly stove to keep his patrons comfortable as they shopped. Kate warmed her hands, relishing the heat.

Ivy, Mr. Thompson's daughter, was arranging a display. She beckoned Kate to come over and look at the items. The two ladies began talking about the upcoming holidays and remembering childhood Christmases.

Kate and Ivy had been school friends but had not maintained communication after Kate had left for New York. Now things were renewing, and it was good to have another single woman to talk to.

An idea struck Kate. "Do you have any scrap pieces of material?"

"Of course; let me show you," Ivy answered, leading the way.

Kate sorted through the material that Ivy placed on the counter. She picked out some pieces and took them to the register where Jonah was setting the paint.

"Do you think your mother has an extra needle and thread?" she asked Jonah. Then she answered her own question. "I shouldn't presume." She glanced at Ivy, who brought over the supplies mentioned.

"These too, I guess." Jonah looked questioningly at Kate and the items on the counter.

"I wasn't expecting you to pay," Kate informed him. "I just remember that most of the toys are 'boy toys' so I thought it would be nice to make some girl things."

Jonah gave her an appreciative grin. "Thank you."

Mr. Thompson tallied up the items, and Jonah slid some coins across the counter. Kate waited for the change and receipt to be handed back. The two men exchanged a quick look, and Jonah thrust the lighter sack into Kate's hands before clomping outside.

"Why didn't you get change back? I saw that you gave Mr. Thompson more than needed, but he didn't make change." Kate hurried to keep up with Jonah's long legs.

Jonah seemed a little hesitant to explain. "For someone in need."

Eying him closely, she began to wonder, *He gives his change to Mr. Thompson to help those who may be short of funds? What kind of man does that? He's not as simple as he appears.*

"Back, Mama! Going downstairs," Jonah bellowed as the front door slammed closed behind him.

"Keep the basement door open!" Jonah's mother called from the kitchen.

Opening the cans of paint, Jonah found a new appreciation for the way the toys were organized. There was a clear area to place the toys once they were painted so they could be taken upstairs to dry easily. As he prepared the paints, he stole glimpses of Kate.

Jonah thought over the conversation about the extra money. A few years earlier, he had seen a father having to make some hard choices regarding his purchases. Jonah had slipped some money into the man's hand and walked away before the man could argue. Now, it was an unspoken agreement between him and Mr. Thompson, whenever there was change from a purchase Jonah made, Mr. Thompson would set it aside for someone he saw that needed it. Jonah considered it an offering to God. He had not told anyone, not even The Club; now Miss Goodwin knew.

Jonah eyed Kate as she worked quietly. A tiny flutter swam through his heart. He took a few deep breaths; the little flutter turned into a swarm of tingles as he watched her.

Kate sat at the small table, stitching a doll blanket. When she had trouble with a knot or something, her face would scrunch up and she exhaled a soft growl. Jonah enjoyed the sight, to see her frustration brought a quiet chortle to his throat.

When her work was smooth, a gentle smile lit her face and Jonah noticed a shine in her eyes. She looked so relaxed and at peace.

*Like a cat basking in the sun. A Katie cat*, he mused directing his attention back to his worktable. *My Katie Cat.* His head popped up from the task in front of him. *Where did that come from?*

He searched the room for some relief from the panicky feeling that settled over him. He looked back at Kate, working silently. The swarm of flutters in his chest became an undeniable pounding.

"Jonah! Kate! Lunch is ready" Mama called from upstairs.

Relived at the interruption, Jonah followed Kate as she walked to the kitchen. Finding two places were set, Jonah raised his brows, questioning his mother.

"I ate as I got yours ready. There's a group of women coming over for a quilting bee tonight," Mama explained. She poured some soup into the bowls, set the salt and pepper in front of Jonah, and then left to the parlor.

Tension filled the room as Jonah and Kate ate silently. In between bites, Kate looked around, uneasiness fluttering in her eyes. Occasionally, their gaze met, and Jonah felt captured by her deep blue eyes. Then Kate would glance away with a light blush, breaking the gaze, but increasing the tension.

After lunch, the two regrettably abandoned the warmth of the kitchen for the cold basement. Silence followed them downstairs. Jonah snatched glances of her as he painted different toys. His mind filled with thoughts of her in his arms, her soft hair sifting through his fingers, her lips warm and gentle, pressing against his.

Jonah rubbed his temples, trying to clear his head. He noticed Kate glancing at him. Did she have the same thoughts? They locked eyes for a moment. A knot rested strangely in his gut; gulping, he imagined her soft touch again. Kate cast her gaze to the ground, forcing a break between them. Jonah watched her worry her bottom lip and sneak a timid peek back at him.

Mama knocked on the open door, poking her head in with a somber look. "You're needed at the Smiths'."

Jonah closed his eyes, nodding his understanding. He was only needed for one reason—someone had died. Together, Kate and Jonah walked upstairs. Jonah went out back to hitch the horses. Kate followed him silently and climbed onto the seat next to him.

"You don't have to go. You could stay here with Mama," Jonah suggested, wanting to protect her from the grief he was about to witness.

"I know. I just feel like I need to go, like I *might* be able to do *something*," she softly pleaded.

Jonah wanted her to go, but at the same time he wanted to shield her from the scene she would witness.

He imagined holding her, Kate's cheek pressed against his chest as she softly cried over the loss, and the comfort he would give with her wrapped in his arms. He looked away, making himself think of the Smith family and what they were going through instead of Kate.

Kate braced herself on the sleigh seat next to Jonah. The swift air rushed through her hair and the runners glided over the snow. She was trying to clear her head and pray for the Smith family. But the way Jonah looked at her sent her heart beating fast.

*I like my men dignified*, she reminded herself. She glanced at Jonah again and bit her lips as her heart jumped. *Don't I?*

Kate moved over closer to the other side of the bench seat. It was best to have as much space between them as she could muster.

The Smith house was a log cabin on a farm outside of town. Inside, the doctor sat with a woman on a sofa, trying to comfort her. "It's not your fault," he said sympathetically.

Doc looked at Jonah and then at a door across the room.

Jonah and Kate entered the bedroom. At the foot of the bed was a cradle. Jonah approached it respectfully. Kate followed. She whimpered at the sight of the baby lying motionless.

*Why hold back?* Kate sniffled softly in her hands, letting the tears fall.

Doc came in. "I don't see any reason this happened. No foul play or poor parenting; just a baby that fell asleep here and woke up in heaven. Still hurts though."

Jonah nodded with a quick sniffle.

Kate looked away as the doctor gathered the baby. He carried the child out as if she were the most precious thing he had seen.

Leaving the house, Jonah met Mr. Smith outside. Kate climbed into the wagon, trying to control the tears. She couldn't hear the conversation, but she saw the tear stains on Mr. Smith's face and heard the muffled sniffles.

Before Kate knew it, she was back at the Layton house, in the basement, staring blindly at the doll blanket in her hands. How could she make this now? Then she remembered some pink satin at the store.

"That's it!" she exclaimed and ran up the stairs, leaving Jonah to himself.

The pink satin she had seen at the store earlier was still available. She bought it and brought it back down to the basement.

"I saw this at the store this morning. I almost got it then but now—" She looked at Jonah with questioning, sorrowful eyes. "Could I make a blanket for—*her*? For the baby?"

Jonah's sad smile warmed Kate's heart. "I think Mrs. Smith would love it."

Kate began to hem the material. As she worked, Jonah picked through the pieces of lumber on the floor.

*He's talking to himself? Odd. He doesn't talk to anyone.* She listened more closely to his deep baritone voice. *Praying! He's praying for the family.*

He continued praying as he measured and sawed the lumber. Kate's heart felt heavier and heavier. She froze at the sound of the first nail being pounded in. Each strike reminded her of the child's life that was no more, of the mother who would face an empty cradle tonight. She couldn't take the noise anymore. She gathered her materials and walked up stairs with no explanation.

In the parlor, Mrs. Layton was preparing her sewing supplies for the bee later that night. Kate sat in a rocking chair and worked on the blanket.

"How did Mr. Layton get started in this business?" Kate inquired.

Mrs. Layton smiled sadly. "When my daughter, Esther, was about twenty, Jonah was about seventeen. Esther had been married a year or so before she had a baby. A beautiful baby girl; born very early. She lived only a few days.

"Jonah felt so bad. The only thing he could do was build the coffin. It was beautiful. He etched the prettiest flowers and butterflies on it. The word spread about his work. People started requesting his services when they were needed. Now, people from town, the settlement across the river, and in other towns will seek his help and his prayers."

Returning to her work on the baby blanket, Kate mulled over the man downstairs. A new understanding of the word gentleman began to form. *A gentleman is polite, but he is also kind and—gentle, like Jonah; I mean Mr. Layton.*

Jonah came upstairs when the clock struck six.

"Friday night," he mumbled.

Kate's brows furrowed in confusion.

"Poker," he continued.

Kate shook her head, still not understanding what he was trying to tell her. Then her father knocked on the front door.

As Mrs. Layton passed Jonah, she quietly instructed, "Complete sentences."

Jonah inhaled deeply and exhaled with a small growl. "Friday night is poker night for The Club. Would you like to come?" He looked around, "Ummm—so Erin can have some company. They're back from their—trip."

Now Kate understood. Father entered the parlor, ready to escort her home. "I'd love to but—" She looked from Jonah to Father and back at Jonah.

"I can give you a ride home," Jonah volunteered, surprising everyone.

Kate looked questioningly at her father. He gave her a quick kiss on the forehead, and stared over her head at Jonah saying, "Not too late."

# CHAPTER 4

# New Information

THE HAMMOND HOUSE
LATER FRIDAY NIGHT

"Kate! Thank goodness. I will need a house full of help to clean all this up." Erin giggled as she set the table with more than enough food for the group. "I guess I got a *little* carried away. We returned this morning, and I immediately began trying my hand at Nanna's recipes. I tried them all. All, except for the bread and the pie. I got those at the bakers."

A large roast, a bowl piled high with mashed potatoes, a gravy boat full of gravy, a basket of dinner rolls, and a dish of green beans graced the table. More food was on the stove, along with a fruit pie warming in the oven.

Jonah pulled out a chair. "Miss Goodwin?" His heart skipped a beat when Kate slipped into the seat with a soft smile. Before anyone else could sit down he planted himself in the seat next to her. *She's wearing that perfume again. I thought I noticed it earlier. That smells nice.*

The group joined hands and bowed heads for prayer. As soon as Jared declared "amen", the men dug into the dishes around them.

"Maybe a plus one ain't such a bad idea," Corbin laughed as he loaded his plate.

Kate smiled, "Mr. Layton will need the strength. Making toys for his cousin's Santa act is harder than I realized."

"Is that what he told you?" Paul asked. "For his cousin?"

Kate beamed at Jonah. "Am I missing something?"

Jonah clenched his jaw and glared at Paul.

"He's shut tight," Kate directed her attention back to Paul. "Please explain."

With an amused grin, Paul raised his brows to Jonah and added a large cut of roast to his plate.

Jonah scowled at him. *Be quiet Paul. I don't like this much attention and you know it.*

Smirking, Paul continued, "Jonah's cousin Josh, comes here the day of our dance, dressed up like Santa. Jonah comes out at some point, so the tots don't think it's him. Oh yeah, the two of them could pass as twins; they even have the same beard. The tykes tell Santa what they want for Christmas and get a toy. When Billington has their Christmas dance, often the same day, Jonah goes there and plays Santa."

Kate beamed at this latest information.

Jonah mixed the mashed potatoes and gravy with a grimace. *Hush up Paul. And when did you start talking so much Katie Cat?*

"I've been making little girl things to give away. It's slow going but there will be a few girls presents," Kate pleasantly announced.

"That's a great idea. I'd love to help!" Erin volunteered.

Kate sat up a bit straighter with a nod and smile. "We should get Ivy involved, too. I've been working on small blankets today. But the three of us, together, will get much more accomplished," Kate noted. Then she beamed at Jonah. "Mr. Layton was such a dear at the mercantile, helping me get the materials and things I needed."

Jonah offered a lopsided, weak smile, but growled inwardly. *Need a change of subject, and now.*

"Paul, any word on the bailiff?" Jonah dipped his roll into the gravy on his plate.

"Naw. There have only been a few small trials since that big one. So it's slipped everyone's mind. We really don't need one right now anyway."

Conversation flowed freely amongst the friends while they ate dinner. Kate fit in well. She talked about her travels in Europe, church, and the changes she noticed in town. She easily became an accepted member of the group.

After dinner, Erin and Kate cleared the table, piling the dishes in the sink to wash later. Then they left for Ivy's house to include her in the plan to make presents.

Jonah started shuffling cards. "Five-card draw. Aces high, jokers wild."

"We haven't said last week's verse yet," Ben protested. "Having a wife that loves God more than she loves me is amazing. She takes time in the morning to read the Bible and listen to me quote the verse from last week. Now, I have a group of friends to hold me accountable and a wife that encourages my time with God. Blessing upon blessing."

Jared grinned. "You think that is what Proverbs talks about? There are more verses than just Proverbs 31."

"I don't know. Right now I'm studying the verses about being a good husband. I should get those down before anything else." Ben pulled out his Bible. "Who's ready?"

The scripture from the previous week was quoted; then each man wrote down his choice for the coming week in a journal. The journal was set aside, a stack of chips given out, and cards dealt.

"You and Miss Goodwin have become chummy," Corbin mentioned, sorting through his hand.

"Only known her a few days. She's quiet, so I let her stay around," Jonah replied quickly.

"Miss Goodwin, quiet?" Paul laughed. "Even as a child she talked nonstop."

"She's quiet around me. That's all I care about." Jonah glared at his hand.

"Is quiet the only reason you let her help?" Ben asked mischievously.

Jonah shrugged, intentionally keeping his eyes on his cards. "She's pretty, I guess."

"I prefer auburn hair," Ben smiled, clearly thinking of Erin.

Corbin shuffled through his cards and absentmindedly said, "Blondes. I've always been partial to blondes."

This was met with chuckles and eye rolls.

"Redheads—redheads with freckles," Jared admitted.

There were guffaws and a sarcastic, "Pastor."

Jared grinned, "Nothing wrong with knowing what attracts us. The problem is when thoughts go too far. It doesn't take long before—"

Ben and Corbin finished his sentence. "—Thoughts become action, and sin takes over."

Jared looked up. "Nice to know you listen."

There was no doubt the men listened to the Sunday morning messages. Sometimes they would have a debate or ask clarification about a Bible verse or part of the sermon. Jared said he loved it when they did this. It meant they were taking God's Word seriously.

"When can we call her Kate? It seemed so natural to call Erin by her given name." Corbin fingered the chips in front of him.

Sorting the cards in his hand, Ben shrugged. "Ask her. Erin asked to be called by her given name. Maybe Miss Goodwin wants that, too. Maybe she likes the formality of her family name."

"Cards?" Paul growled, redirecting the conversation.

Jonah was grateful for the distraction. He knew he could count on Paul to get the fellas back on cards, even if Paul had spilled the beans about his playing Santa.

Later that evening, on the way home, Kate tucked the thick blanket around her lap in the sleigh, appreciating the warmth and the time alone with Jonah. In the basement, he was focused on the toys. Now, she had his attention and wanted to get to know him better. She had learned a topic they could talk about, his Santa act.

"When you play Santa, what do you do with your beard? In the pictures, he has a white beard, yours is a dark blond. He often has a large belly, also. How do you add that?"

"Mama made me fake whiskers that covers mine. A belly is sewn in the suit."

*A grown man calling his mother Mama makes him sound like a little boy. But he's so much more than that.*

She searched her mind for more things to talk about. This would be harder than she thought. *He just needs to be pulled out of his shell, and I'm the one who can do it. I love challenges and I love the social life. He just doesn't know what he's missing.*

"Did Erin and Ben tell you about their trip? They went to Boise. Have you ever visited there?"

Jonah shook his head. "Just to see Esther."

"I was in New York for finishing school. Erin went to one in Philadelphia. While they were in Boise, on their trip, Erin got a manicure. It's all the rage in Europe. They went to an opera and some law library. Erin became lost in the rows of books. After that, Ben made her hold his hand, so they didn't get separated again. Can you imagine? Holding hands in public? She said her schoolmarms would be screaming right now if they knew she had done that." Kate laughed, eyeing Jonah. His shoulders were bunched up near his ears and his chin was lowered. *There is that turtle Mother mentioned. I will pull that turtle out of his shell; I know I will.*

She changed the subject to the winter dance and continued her rambling. "I have been working with the Ladies Auxiliary for the winter dance. Things have grown since I was little. We used to have a dance, and that was it. Now it's the dance, the Santa visit and holiday treats.

"Cook is teaching me how to make cookies for Christmas. She is wonderful in the kitchen.

"You should have seen the decorations in Europe. They were beautiful. Have you ever been to Europe? Anywhere?"

Jonah shook his head with a tight grimace. The sleigh stopped at her house. He helped her out, the grimace becoming more of a frown. "Good evening, Miss Goodwin." The horses were snapped into a quick trot back to his place.

Kate waved goodnight and wondered if he had seen it since he had left in such a hurry. *Soon, I will get him to open up—soon.*

SUNDAY, DECEMBER 7
RAVEN CREST CHURCH

"—Amen." Jared closed his Bible. The members began to shuffle out of their seats. Mothers were holding babies. Fathers instructed children about proper church behavior. Adolescent boys were dashing outside to play in the fresh snow. Young girls talked in groups, giggling, and pointing behind their hands.

Jonah stepped outside. He had waited inside longer than he usually did. Ignoring the uncomfortable ride Friday night, he was hoping to help Kate with her coat, but she was talking with a group of ladies, and he needed some fresh air.

A few deep breaths cleared his lungs and his head. *Thank you, God. I stayed in there longer this time, and I didn't feel so flustered. I just need to focus on You, not on the crowd.*

*Kate talked so much Friday night that it was nerve wracking. I want to get to know her. I enjoy her company and her liveliness, but sometimes the talking gets to be too much and I —*

He turned at the small tug on his coat.

"Mr. Layton?" A little boy about five or six tugged at his coat again.

"Yes?" *I can talk to little ones a lot easier than adults.*

"Are you Santa?"

"Why would you think that?" Jonah raised his brows.

"Because my cousin Herb," The little boy grabbed another boy and pulled him over. "He says you are, and I say you ain't."

Jonah knelt down in the soft snow and began forming a ball. "Tell me why you think what you think."

The boys watched him closely. "Well, ummm, I say no because Santa lives in the South Pole."

"The North Pole, Johnny." Herb pushed his cousin.

"If he lives in the North Pole then it can't be Mr. Layton." Johnny pushed back. "What are you doing?"

"Building a snowman. I could use two sticks for his arms." He began another mound of snow.

The boys ran to some bare trees and yanked two low hanging branches down.

"Here. Anything else?" Herb and Johnny jumped in anticipation.

Jonah set the mound on top of the first mound and began another. "We need eyes, a nose and something to make a smile."

The boys ran off to find the needed items. A laugh nearby caught Jonah's attention. *That sounds like—It is, it's her laugh. Her laugh sounds like sleigh bells, almost a tinkle, not a laugh.*

Kate met his gaze and tenderly smiled at him. Captured in her eyes, a soft warmth flooded his heart. She was surrounded by older adolescent girls who were all talking and giggling. But she was all that mattered, her smile, her eyes, her gentle ways, and the way she wanted to help anyone in need.

*She's helping those girls. She is giving them instruction on how to be a godly woman, but not a stuffy woman. Now she's getting them involved in the winter dance. She's encouraging them to pray about what to bring to the dance. How does she do that?*

Another tug brought his attention back to the boys and the snowman.

"Mr. Layton. What are you making now? That's too big for a head." Johnny wrinkled his nose.

Jonah chuckled at the large mound of snow in his hands. "Watch this." He pushed the mound on top, placed the two twigs in the middle pointing down. He dotted two eyes with pebbles on the bottom ball. Then he drew a nose and used the last of the rocks to make an upside down smile.

Johnny hopped and clapped his hands. "He's standing on his head!"

"Another one. Let's make another one!" Herb insisted.

"Sorry fellas. My mama is calling me for lunch. I suggest you listen for your mama too. After all, Santa knows if you are being good or not."

Tuesday morning, December 9
The Layton kitchen

Jonah's knee bobbed as he glanced at the clock one more time.

Mama drained the bacon grease into a cup on the stove. "This will make good seasoning for dinner."

*She should be here any time now. Did she get the same feeling that I did when we looked at each other Sunday? Would she agree to a match with me?*

Both knees began to bounce. *I've only really known her a few days; why am I thinking about a match?*

His mother rested her hand on his leg. "You're making the whole kitchen shake." With a small smile, she added, "Kate will be here soon, don't worry. I can see it in her eyes."

Jonah exhaled deeply. "It's just—"

Mama rubbed his knee. "I know; I remember."

Kate came dressed in a warm, thick sweater of blue and green plaid with a matching skirt.

"I think I'm ready for the cold," she giggled.

Jonah cast a glance at his mother, who smiled, lightly amused. He led Kate to the basement, making sure to keep the door open.

He didn't want any misunderstandings. This way anyone could walk in without notice, or she could easily leave.

Kate sat in her usual spot and began sewing. She also began talking.

"Yesterday afternoon, at the funeral, there was no graveside service. That would be unbearable for Mrs. Smith to watch her baby getting lowered to the ground.

"After the funeral, I met Ivy and Erin at Marcy's Diner. We had the most wonderful dish. I think it was a hickory-smoked ham. Pastor met us to talk about Christmas morning. The Ladies Auxiliary is letting us lead the way with that event. We are planning to set up a Christmas tree for the whole town at the church. It will be bare, and we will hang gifts on it, presents that anyone wants to give. Young men to sweethearts or husbands to wives. It will be a fun surprise. Oh, and we will have bags of candy for the children too. But it will take some doing to get it ready. Erin said Ben may be busy so don't count on him, but I said you would help of course."

Jonah's head popped up. *I'm helping? When did that happen? I gotta get out of that and quick.*

Kate stood up and walked around the room, patting her arms, and talking. Now she was talking about how cold it was in the basement.

She walked up to the large double-door closet "What's in here?" she asked as she reached for a handle.

"Don't! Don't open that!" Jonah demanded.

Kate turned, surprised. "Why? What's in here?" Her hand rested on the handle like she was considering opening the door.

"When it's frozen outside, we can't dig—resting places."

Kate knitted her brows, trying to understand. Slowly, realization dawned. "You mean there's—coffins in there—*coffins with—with— someone in them?*"

"Just one right now," he answered sadly. By the end of winter there will be more. He knew that from experience.

Kate curled her lip in revulsion.

"I—think—I—hear your mother." She rapidly gathered her things and hurried up the stairs.

Pacing the basement, Jonah cupped the back of his head. *Help me, Lord. There are too many feelings. I can't sort them all out. She fills my every thought. I want to protect her from sad things like the closet, but I also want her to stop talking so much. I'm starting to get a headache from all this.*

Mama's call interrupted his thoughts, "Jonah! Josh is here. Come get lunch."

He trudged up the stairs and kicked the basement door closed. "How are Ingrid and the girls?"

"She's still the most wonderful woman I know." Josh bragged, pulling his chair closer to the kitchen table and began a proud papa ramble about his daughters.

Without thinking, Jonah pulled out a chair for Kate next to his. Kate perched in her seat, batted her lashes at Jonah, and then bowed her head for prayer.

"Josh, will you do the honors?" Mama bowed her head also.

"Yes Ma'am." He thanked the Lord for the food and the opportunity to share His love through the toy giveaway.

After the amen, Kate poured a dipper full of soup into a bowl. "Jon—Mr. Layton, would you like more?"

Yes please." Another dipper was added to the bowl. "Thank you, Kate. I mean Miss Goodwin."

Kate smiled sweetly, "Kate, please." Batting her lashes a few times, she asked shyly, "May I call you Jonah?"

Again, he was lost in those deep blue eyes. Words refused to come out; all he could do was grin and nod.

Returning her attention to the table, she poured Josh a bowl and then Jonah's mother her own bowl of soup. Last, she served herself.

"Mrs. Layton, this soup is tasty. I am baking a cake tonight. Can I bring it tomorrow?"

"Of course, dear."

"You're coming back tomorrow? I thought after what happened—" Jonah held his spoon over his bowl, surprised.

Kate smiled shyly. "I understand about the closet, I think. I also think I overacted. I'm sorry. God is teaching me new ways of thinking, and I am trying to hear Him better."

*I knew there was more to her than what meets the eye. Listening to God, seeking Him, thinking of others.*

Jonah thoughtlessly dipped his roll in his soup, captured by Kate and her smile. Slowly he raised the roll close to his lips. He couldn't take his eyes off Kate and her gentle ways. Before the roll entered his mouth, he began dabbing it in his soup again. A few more dunks into the bowl and he absent-mindedly raised the bread again. A large hunk of soggy bread dropped into his bowl splattering soup.

Jonah cleared his throat trying to ignore Josh's chuckle. He forced his gaze downward and dropped the roll in his bowl, he cut it up with his spoon to finish eating, trying to get his thoughts back to the table conversation between Josh and Mama.

Josh snorted a small laugh at him. Then, under the table, he kicked Jonah. Jonah kicked back and growled quietly to Josh.

"Kate dear, the men need to talk downstairs. Can you help me up here? Some of the heavy lifting is just too much for me and my old back," Mama said.

"Yes Ma'am." Kate modestly smiled at Jonah. "What is your favorite cake? Maybe I can make that tonight."

"Velvet. But I think that takes cocoa, doesn't it Mama?"

"Yes. But you also like angel food. That recipe is simple compared to velvet cakes."

Kate began to clear the table. "I may have to start with the simpler one." She glanced over her shoulder, gasping, "Oh, Mrs. Layton! I have taken over. I dished the soup. Now I'm clearing the table. I didn't mean to overstep. I'm so sorry."

"No need to worry, dear. I have enjoyed being waited on."

Josh slid his chair back. "Jonah, we need to work things out. And I want to see what you've done so far. I can't be put to shame."

In the basement, Josh pulled out a cigar and clipped the end. He struck a match on the sole of his boot and inhaled deeply. "Want one?"

Jonah shook his head. "I prefer the smell of pipe tobacco. Papa used to sport a pipe, but I never could get accustomed to smoking one myself."

"Ingrid says they are a filthy habit. She makes me smoke outside. I don't know if they are or not, but I do enjoy a good stogie to help me relax. And what is going on with you? I've never seen you this taken with a woman."

Jonah dropped on a stack of planks. "I don't know. I can't stop thinking about her but sometimes she drives me daft. She talks so much. She likes parties and—well, everything I don't care for."

So, is it just physical? You're just attracted to her looks?"

"No. There's so much more to her than just being pretty. She went to the Smith funeral even though she didn't know them. She wanted to help them as much as she could. She made a blanket for the baby and one just like it for Mrs. Smith. She said it was a gentle reminder of how beautiful Mrs. Smith's baby is. She gets involved in social gatherings, but it's usually undertakings to help the town, like the Christmas celebration. Sunday, she was getting the young ladies to pray about what to bring to the dance. She said prayer is for everything, not just big things. She will be up there helping Mama even though she has never done work like that before—"

"I've never heard you talk this much. Are you falling in love?"

Jonah shrugged. "How do you know the difference between love and infatuation? And you know how I get around women."

"I can't explain how to tell the difference. You just know it when you get there. And why do you have such a tough time talking to women? Did something happen when you were a lad?"

Jonah rubbed his face. "Yes. I was laughed at a lot. First, the scars and lisp. I was a little boy then. But as an adolescent, I was laughed at too—mostly by girls. I don't know why but I was."

"Girls laugh at everything. That's just what they do. And I know why you were laughed at. You were sort of a creepy young man."

"What? What do you mean creepy? I stayed to myself or my friends."

"And you read those Edgar Allen Poe books a lot. They were your favorite. You would chuckle when you read those horror stories."

"They are so ridiculous, they're funny. But I don't do that anymore. With the vocation I have, it seems rude."

"Most women don't know you've changed. Maybe there needs to be more changes in you. Maybe Miss Goodwin is the one to help with that. Is she worth changing for?"

"Something to think about, I guess. I am trying. Not only for her, but I'm trying to trust God, too," Jonah shrugged. "I thought we needed to talk about the toy giveaway. When's your dance?" Josh began to ramble about the toys he had made and the Billington dance. Jonah leaned back, forcing himself to listen to Josh. But Kate and the idea of changing kept intruding.

*I need to pray about this. It's too much on my own.*

# CHAPTER 5

# The Quiet Kate

FRIDAY, DECEMBER 12

"Knock, knock." Kate tapped softly on the Layton's front door.

Jonah's heart did a crazy flip at the sound of Kate's voice.

He rushed to the front door, but before he could open it, Mama called out, "Come in! I'm in the kitchen! Jonah's headed to the basement just now"

"Time is getting so close. I need to get those toys finished." Jonah trembled slightly, closing the door behind Kate. He was hoping for a smile or a flutter from those big blue eyes.

He wasn't disappointed. Jonah gulped, and his heart beat wildly at the coy smile and lash flutter.

Kate swung a basket of scrap material on her arm and carried a covered plate of goodies. "I have some doll blankets to finish, too. Between the two of us there should be plenty of toys. Erin and Ivy's help has been invaluable."

Mama took the offered plate and peeked under the cloth. "Mmmm! What are these? They look delightful!"

"They are called cupcakes. Cook found them in a cookbook, and I had to try them. After my disaster frosting the large cake, I thought these might be a little easier." She lowered her head bashfully, with a sheepish smile. "I never did bring that cake over. It was too embarrassing."

"No need to fret dear. We all have had our blunders in the kitchen. Now, I will set them over here, and we can try them after lunch." Mama settled the plate of cupcakes on the kitchen counter.

Kate led the way to the basement. Before she sat down, she began describing different cakes and cookies she had made with Cook the day before. She talked about her failures and successes, her preferences, and her dislikes.

*She keeps talking. My head is pounding. I worked on the Smith bill until late last night. He's supposed to be here sometime today. I need time to pray about it. Help me, Lord.*

Mama knocked on the open door. "Jonah, Mr. Smith is here to see you. Kate, could you come upstairs for a bit, please?"

Kate glared at Jonah. She cast a sad frown to Mr. Smith. "Of course I will."

After Jonah settled business with Mr. Smith, Kate rejoined Jonah in the basement.

"I was fairly upset with you when I went upstairs. I thought 'How could he make that family pay for such a thing.' Then your mother explained more. She told me that will be the last thing Mr. Smith will ever be able to give his little girl. She also said that you pray about how much to charge. If you feel the price will be too much of a burden, you adjust it. What made you start doing that?"

"Just wanna help is all," Jonah mumbled.

"You're a great blessing to those in mourning," Kate gazed at him fondly.

Jonah was torn. He wanted her to stop talking, to sit down and work quietly so he could steal glances at her and catch her watching him. He also wanted his privacy. She knew about the Santa roll, she volunteered him to help on Christmas Eve, she knew about his change at Mr. Thompson's, and now she knew about his business arrangements. The fellas at the Club may know most of this, but they didn't talk about it. These were his private decisions, between him and God, no one else.

*I want to know her better, but I also want my quiet. I want my quiet Katie Cat.*

Mama called from the basement door, "It is lunch time. I have prepared a small lunch since you are going to the Club tonight."

Upstairs, Jonah pulled out a seat for Kate. *I used to laugh at men who did this. Now I do it without thinking, just hoping for a smile from her.* He was granted the winning smile, and his heart melted. *Maybe the talking isn't so bad after all. I just wish there was less of it.*

A few quick taps at the back door surprised them all. Jonah's heart dropped. *That usually means only one thing.*

Mama answered the knock and escorted Mr. Thompson to the table.

Mr. Thompson smiled broadly to Jonah, "No need to fret. I came by for something other than your—um—services."

"Would you like some stew?" Mama offered.

"No thank you. I just had Marcy's for lunch. I did come by to discuss something with Jonah." Mr. Thompson pulled out a chair and raised his brows to Jonah.

Jonah nodded, inviting Mr. Thompson to sit down.

Mama buttered some bread. "Should Miss Goodwin and I leave? We can take our lunch in the parlor if you wish."

Mr. Thompson shook his head. "No, there is no reason to leave. But if you get bored and decide to go, I understand."

Kate handed Jonah a piece of buttered bread and passed the salt and pepper to him.

*She knows I always add salt and pepper to my stew. And she is listening, not talking. She can be quiet when she wants to.*

"So, Jonah, several of the business men in town met at Marcy's to-day. We have been talking about the idea of a chamber of commerce here in Raven Crest. Do you have any thoughts on the subject?"

"What's a chamber of commerce?" Jonah furrowed his brows trying to understand.

"The business owners in town would meet and discuss any issues that might be affecting our businesses. We would elect a committee to bring concerns or suggestions to the town council."

"What brought this on?"

"The saloon. The town council looked at how it would affect the town and how it would bring in more taxes, but no one asked the business owners about our concerns. So far, we haven't had any problems, but that could change. What if another saloon wants to come to our town, one that might bring . . ." He glanced at the women, ". . . other business with them."

Mama stood with a quiet nod. "Kate, darling, let's to go to the parlor."

Kate followed. "What other business are they talking about? Why would more business be concerning?"

After the door closed, Mr. Thompson shook his head with a small laugh. "I really don't want to be part of that conversation."

Jonah chuckled and shook his head. "I do like the idea of a chamber, but why are you asking me?"

"You run an important business. You offer a service and sell . . . products."

"If the wrong businesses came to town, and the wrong men, my services might be needed more. I don't want that. Aye, I think it's a good idea. What would be expected of me?"

"Just come to the first meeting. It will be after the New Year. We will all talk and decide what the next steps are then. Right now, we are just seeing if there is an interest."

"Corbin. Have you talked to him?"

"He is next on my list."

"You should stay and have one of Kate's little cakes. They do look good. Mama! Done!"

The women filed into the kitchen. Kate glanced at the men and blushed crimson. She busied herself with her small cakes, trying to hide her embarrassment.

A plate was set in front of everyone, with a little frosted cake on it.

Mr. Thompson took a hesitant bite. "Mmmm. These are good. The last cake my Ivy made was rather . . . crunchy, and . . . flat."

"Crunchy? How is a cake crunchy?" Kate nibbled on her piece.

"Egg shells. And she dropped the clothes iron on the stove after it started to rise, so it fell flat. She is good at many things, but cooking is a challenge for her."

Kate smiled. "She always hated helping in the kitchen. She used to say that it was dull and took no imagination at all. But she did make sure all of our dolls were properly cared for and bandaged. I'm not surprised she became a nurse." Kate carried the empty plates to the sink.

"Mrs. Layton, shall I assist you or Jonah?"

"You should finish up with the Christmas gifts before it gets too late. Good afternoon, Mr. Thompson." Mama smoothed her apron and turned to the sink for washing.

Mr. Thompson left for the mill, and Jonah went downstairs to finish the toys.

Kate followed and began her monologue for most of the afternoon.

Jonah tried to concentrate on the boat in front of him. But his head began to throb. *I can whittle the animals in the evening after she leaves. The soldiers are made, they just need to be painted . . . did she just ask me something?*

"Oh, Jonah! Look, you just nailed the mast on the bottom of the boat. You should be more careful." Kate giggled.

Jonah shook his head. *I did! I just nailed the mast to the bottom of the boat. I gotta get my mind on this. How do I get her to stop talking so much?*

Later, he and Kate walked to Erin and Ben's house. The Club was meeting at the Hammond house, more frequently, at Erin's insistence. Erin said she loved cooking for them and wanted to give Mrs. Layton a break.

The Club gladly accepted the change. There was more room and more food, compared to Corbin and Jared's places. And at the Laytons', the men felt like little boys needing to keep company manners when Mrs. Layton would enter the kitchen.

After dinner, Erin kissed Ben goodbye, informing him they were going to Ivy's. They were starting a Bible study and then working on toys for Christmas.

The women left, and Jared began to tell them about the plans the ladies were making for Christmas morning.

"Shh. I just want quiet. Just for a few minutes," Jonah begged.

Corbin chuckled. "Sounds like trouble in paradise."

"She won't stop talking. Well, if there's food in her mouth, she's quiet, but she doesn't eat much so . . ." Jonah let the sentence hang. "I just want a quiet Kate like she used to be before she got comfortable around me."

"Talk to her; tell her what's wrong," Ben suggested.

Corbin had another idea. "Try leading the conversation. Ask her questions, so she is talking about something you're interested in."

Jonah rubbed his temples. "Think I could kiss her quiet?" knowing the answer before he asked.

"I don't suggest trying," Jared said. "But you've got it bad, huh?"

"I'll get over it if she keeps talking. Ben and Erin made everything look so easy. You never had any problems."

Ben laughed. "There's no such thing. Every couple has problems they have to work on. Erin and I are still working things out. We just have to talk to each other. Is Kate worth talking to?"

Jonah tented his fingers over his mouth and forced a few deep breaths. "I used to enjoy listening to her talk. But she only talked a little. Now I feel like I can hardly think because she talks so much. I want her to be her, but I need some quiet too. I'm still praying about it."

They went back to the cards, leaving Jonah to figure things out. Some things a man must take care of on his own, and this was one of them.

"Knock, knock! Ivy, are you home? Mr. Thompson?" Kate tapped on the Thompsons' house door. *Let Ivy lead the meeting. I suggested it, Erin organized it, and now Ivy is leading the study. I don't always have to be in charge,* Kate reminded herself.

Mr. Thompson answered the door, inviting Kate and Erin into the parlor. "Please come in. Ivy's been looking forward to this. She is in the store right now, double-checking the receipts with the cash drawer. How have you two been? Mrs. Hammond, marriage suits you well, I see. Miss Goodwin?"

Erin smiled softly. "I am enjoying married life. And it is fun preparing the Christmas celebration with Ivy and Kate."

"Preparing the Christmas gifts with my friends is wonderful. Things are different here than they used to be. How long has Ivy been back?" Kate placed her basket on the floor near a rocker.

"A little more than a year. After Mother passed, she decided to stay. I wish Mother could see her grow in Christ the way she is doing."

The door between the store and the parlor opened. "I wish she could see it too. But I know she is busy in heaven, praising God. Are we ready?" Ivy smiled sadly at the mention of her mother.

Mr. Thompson bowed out, leaving the ladies alone.

Erin settled in a needlepoint chair. "I know you have been back for a while, and I'm sorry I didn't pursue our friendship more. First, your mother was ill. Then, I thought you were going back to New York. Soon, I was busy with Miss Burns and then the businesses. But I'm so glad Kate started this. Now, we can all be friends, better than we used to be."

"I would like that so much. I help Father in the store most days. But some days I am helping Nurse Meadows. All our friends from school are busy with children and husbands." Ivy flashed a smile at Erin. "I know, you have Ben now, but somehow this feels different. I am so grateful to have friends who are trying to grow in the Lord like I am. I think this study is the next step for me."

Erin nodded. "I agree. You do well leading talks and studies. Kate? You've been quiet. Is something wrong?"

Kate rocked slowly in a rocking chair. "No. I am just letting others lead instead of me. The other day, Jonah's cousin came to the Layton house. I found myself serving the whole family. I took charge and it should have been Mrs. Layton. I'm trying to learn how to let others shine. I think this is a good opportunity for Ivy. Remember when we were young girls? I wanted a game about boys, Erin started it, and Ivy kept it going. What was that game 'Kick or Marry'?"

Ivy laughed. "Yes, we would pick two boys and challenge another girl to choose. She had to say whom she would rather kick or marry. Beverly would often choose to marry George. And she did! I helped Nurse Meadows delivery their second child last week."

"I don't think I ever chose Ben to marry, that is not until recently." Erin smiled.

Kate shook her head. "Was his name mentioned? He's older than us. By the time we were playing that game, he was probably preparing for college. We were off to finishing school not long after that."

"So, now we can use The Club. Who would you kick or marry?" Erin grinned slyly at Kate.

Kate frowned. "Kicking is mean, so no one. As for marry, I choose the man God has planned for me. I'm sorry. That game was funny when we were silly young girls, but I need to set my attentions on God right now, not men." *Especially not Jonah. I want to kick him when he's being so withdrawn and maybe someday marry him? I can't think about that, I need to think about God.*

Ivy turned pages in her Bible and named the verse she would read. "Are we ready?" Kate and Erin nodded. They began to sew, letting Ivy read the verses. Soon, a conversation about the scripture began.

*Thank you, Lord. I need this right now,* Kate prayed silently. Kate enjoyed the evening with friends and work until Erin declared it time to go. The thought of riding home next to Jonah sent a soft patter through Kate's heart. She closed her eyes. *Help me, Lord. Help me be the woman You want me to be, not the flirt I was taught to be.*

CHAPTER 6

# The Dance

Jonah dipped a rag in paint thinner. Another mistake. The dance was Saturday, and he was far behind. He had been called to Billington yesterday for another family in mourning. When he got home, he found Mama in tears. Yesterday would have been her and Papa's thirty-fifth wedding anniversary. After comforting Mama, he stayed up late preparing the coffin. Exhaustion pounded at his temples.

*Quiet. All I want is a few minutes of quiet,* Jonah silently growled.

"What do you think? Should we have candy bags in a bowl to hand out to children when they come in, or should we tie them on the tree and give them like gifts?" Kate asked expecting an answer.

Jonah heard her talking but didn't listen to what she was saying. He was cleaning off another mistake, and this one horse was taking more time than it should.

"Jonah?" Kate called, demanding his attention.

He looked up, not hiding the annoyance. "What?"

"Should the bags of candy be on the tree or in a bowl?" Hands on her hips, Kate obviously expected his support.

"Bowl," he answered, unsure of what she was talking about. He went back to work on the horse, trying to paint a face on the little animal.

"That's what I think. Then we don't have to worry about anyone being overlooked, and the children can eat the candy while they are waiting for their gifts. But Erin thinks the—"

"Don't you ever stop talking?" Jonah bellowed, realizing he had just given the horse a purple nose.

Kate's eyes widened in surprise and hurt.

Jonah was furious. He had work to do, his head throbbed, and he was getting further and further behind. "You used to be so quiet. Now all you do is talk. Just be quiet for a few minutes, please! If you have to talk that much, go talk to Mama." He brushed the sting of tears away from his eyes. "And stop volunteering me for things."

Kate's lips puckered, eyes brimming. "I only volunteered you once! You might like it if you gave it a try! And you won't have to listen to me anymore!" She rushed upstairs, banging the door shut after her.

Closing his eyes, Jonah took several deep breaths. He had hurt her. He had spoken out of anger. He knew he needed to apologize. He knew he needed to make things right, but he had quiet. He could get some work done in peace, and then at lunch, he would apologize. It could wait until then. Right now, he needed to work. He needed his quiet.

*Lord, I'm sorry. I spoke out of anger. I'm so tired. I have given of myself until there is nothing left. I feel like a ghost wandering around with more and more demanded of me. I need Your help.*

He let the tears fall, until he had none left. Wiping his eyes, he faced the stack of toys still needing paint. *There's so much. But all I can do is one at a time . . . just one at a time.*

He caught a glimpse of planks in the corner. *And another coffin. I need to build that soon, too. I will do that after dinner tonight.*

Jonah worked in silence until his stomach started growling and could no longer be ignored.

*Why hasn't Mama called for lunch yet?*

He left the toys in the basement and headed upstairs. Jonah was sure to find Mama and Kate sitting at the table talking. He entered the kitchen; the smell of fresh bread and cookies filled the air. Mama was at the stove, by herself, stirring last night's soup.

Fresh flour clung to the table in places where Mama had been kneading the bread. It was baking day, and the toy giveaway was Saturday night during the winter dance. Mama was busy with all the festivities.

She turned around with a smile that told him she knew about his argument with Kate.

"Here's some soup. You can have one cookie, but I'm saving the rest for the dance. The bread will be ready for dinner."

Jonah grabbed two cookies, sulking at Kate's empty seat.

Mama swatted his hand. "I said one!" Then with a warning stare, she added, "Do you want to tempt me?"

That was her question when he was young and trying her patience. As a child that meant the paddle was close at hand, and she wasn't afraid to use it.

He smiled and shook his head. Then he sat down, trying to inconspicuously look for Kate.

"I took her home," Mama nonchalantly informed him.

Jonah's shoulders slumped and his face fell a little. Mama sat down and prayed for the meal. She began to eat quietly, occasionally glancing at Jonah. She shifted in her seat and cleared her throat. Jonah glanced up through his brows.

Mama slid the salt and pepper to Jonah, asking, "Is there something you would like to talk about?"

"No," Jonah answered bluntly.

Mama would help if he let her. Mama loved getting involved in such matters. But she would just tell him to go talk to Kate, to go and apologize like he was taught to do.

Jonah mulled over the idea. *I'll go tonight. It might be too cold tonight. Maybe tomorrow, if I'm caught up on work. Well, I'll probably*

*see her tomorrow night at the Club. That's it for sure, unless . . .*
Jonah could feel the procrastination sneaking in. He sighed. *Next
time I see her, I'll talk to her.*

**FRIDAY, DECEMBER 19**

Jonah glared at the world as he stomped to Ben and Erin's
place alone, his dark mood hanging over him like a cloud. *She
didn't come over today, and I don't blame her. How could I have
been so rude to her? I've never spoken like that to anyone, not even
my sister. I need to apologize. But . . . but . . . but I'm procrastinating
and making things worse. It's all my fault.*

The fellas and Erin were gathered around the hitching post,
admiring Jared's new horse.

"Revelation," Jared laughed. "I call him Revelation because it
was a true revelation to me when I realized how much time I spent
walking to farms or finding a horse to borrow. At the Simmons, I
hesitated to use a stall. I knew my board was a gift of theirs to God
and didn't want to take advantage. But now I have the stable out
back at the parsonage, so I don't need to fret."

The men laughed; glad Jared was able to purchase such a fine
specimen. Now that he lived at Ben's old place, he was finding new
freedoms. He had saved enough money for the horse and was enjoying the liberties of a bachelor's life.

"Are you getting settled in? Mother said it took all week to get
it cleaned and my things brought over," Ben inquired.

Jared stroked Revelation. "Yes. It seemed too large when I first
moved in, and I've only been there a few weeks, but I'm filling up the
rooms faster than I thought I would. There's enough space that I can
have an office for preparing sermons if I can't work at the church,
and another room for whatever I need it for. I am learning to cook
for myself, and I've been going to Marcy's Diner more often too."

Jonah listened with a small scowl. "It's cold; I'm going in," he
grumbled. *Don't cry again, you big baby. She won't be there.*

The rest of the group followed him in and sat down to eat.

"Is Kate coming?" Corbin innocently asked.

"How should I know?" Jonah frowned and pulled his coat around himself tighter, complaining, "I'm cold."

Jared moved his plate across the table. "You can sit here."

After changing seats, he glowered, "Too hot now."

"You could take your coat off," Ben suggested.

Jonah glared at him and took his coat off. "Not better."

Erin tried to bring up a more pleasant conversation. "I've been thinking of having the girls over here for Bible study while you fellas play poker."

Jared and Corbin smiled, nodding their approval. Paul shrugged with a twisted grin.

Jonah hunched down deeper, fighting a pout. "That's not what the Bachelor's Club does." *Kate will come, then what? I would have to face her. I don't know if I can do that.*

Erin looked at Ben with concern and glanced at Jonah. Ben shrugged a little, quickly looking at the door with raised brows. Erin gave a sympathetic half smile and began clearing the table.

"I'll take care of these later." Then she flung a scarf around her neck, fastened a cap on her head, and wrapped her coat around her before she faced the cold outside.

Ben started shuffling the cards. Paul poured himself a cup of coffee. Jared and Corbin folded their arms, waiting to hear what was wrong.

"So, are you gonna tell us what happened, or do we beat it out of you?" Ben asked.

Jonah looked around the table, getting the same stern look from each man. He could either tell, or they would "help" him tell. He gave up and slumped over with his head in his hands.

"She wouldn't stop talking. So, I told her —"

"Oh no," Corbin's shoulders sagged.

"You didn't say . . . I can't even say those words it's so wrong." Ben shook his head.

"Shut up?" Jared wrinkled his brow, concern etching his face.

Paul sat back shaking his head. "That's just plain rude."

Jonah dropped his head on his folded arms. "No! I didn't say that! I told her to be quiet. I told her to go talk to Mama. And to stop volunteering me for things. But I spoke out of anger. I was so tired. I had so much to do, and she just kept talking. I needed my quiet. What do I do?" He looked at his friends, hoping for some answer to his dilemma. "Why can't she just stay upstairs with Mama. I could see her when I come up for lunch and at dinner. Shoot, she could stay there all evening then."

"She'd have to live there for that to work. Are you ready for this?" Ben held up his left hand and rubbed his wedding band. He was the only man in town with a band. Ben said if men could wear class rings and social rings, he could wear a ring to show everyone his love for Erin.

Jonah looked at the band. "Doesn't matter. She won't have anything to do with me now."

"Talk to her!" Corbin, Ben, and Jared said in unison.

Paul kept his arms folded in front of him. "Batchin' it looks better and better."

Jonah looked around the table. "Should I go now? What if she cries?" His shoulders sagged deeper, "What if I cry? What do I say besides I'm sorry? Sorry just isn't good enough."

"Best wait. Erin's talking to her right now. Take tonight to get your head straight, and talk to her tomorrow," Ben instructed.

This fit in well with Jonah's procrastination. He agreed, postponing the inevitable.

THE GOODWIN HOUSE

Kate roughly flipped a page in a book, pretending to read.

"That poor book may not take much more of that reading Kate," Father gently rebuked.

"You've been like this for two days now. Mrs. Layton brought you home early yesterday, and you haven't left at all today. Do you want to talk about it?" Mother asked, concern filling her voice.

"No." Kate answered gruffly, turning another page in the book, and then dropping it hard on a nearby side table. She folded her arms and glowered, thinking of Jonah and the argument in the basement yesterday.

A knock sent Kate rushing to the door hoping it was Jonah, ready to apologize. Her heart dropped at seeing Erin and Ivy. "Oh, it's you. Come in." *What did you expect? He hasn't talked to you since that awful day, yesterday. He probably never will again,* Kate bemoaned silently.

"Nice seeing you, too," Erin teased. "Let's go to your room, so we can talk."

Kate led them upstairs and into her room. Then she fell face up on the bed and began to cry.

Erin and Ivy found seats, waiting until the crying slowed down.

"Talk," Ivy instructed.

"Are you going to tell me to be quiet?" Kate asked through her tears and hiccups.

Erin and Ivy looked astonished.

"Let's hear it," Erin requested.

"He told me to be quiet. He said I was talking too much. He said I have to stop volunteering him for things."

"Jonah does like his quiet. Were you talking a lot?" Erin asked.

Kate brushed away some tears. "Does it matter? How can I have anything to do with him now? I just wanted to get to know him better."

"He was wrong talking to you that way," Ivy comforted. "But forgiveness can be hard, too."

"Do you think I should forgive him?" Kate questioned unsure.

"I think you need to decide that for yourself. And what have you volunteered him for?" Erin asked.

"Just the Christmas Eve decorating. I know he will love it if he tries it."

Erin stroked Kate's hair. "The way you talked at the meeting; he had already agreed. Maybe you should ask him before you sign him up for something. But he does need to apologize for how he spoke. Do you need to apologize for anything?"

"It's something to think about, I guess," Kate moaned. A new set of tears burst. "I've been waiting for an apology, candy, or something but he hasn't said a word. How can I care about him so much and feel so mad at the same time?"

"The only person that can make me that mad is Ben. It hurts more when he makes mistakes, because I love him so much. And it's the same for him. When I get cross or take my frustrations out on him, it hurts him more than anything. You need to decide, do you hate what Jonah said, or do you have bad feelings toward *him*? How much do you want him to change to fit you, and how much of him are you willing to accept? We all come to a bridge like that. A decision needs to be made about the future. A future with him or without him. Him and all his flaws." Erin continued stroking Kate's hair.

"I don't want to change him; I want him to change for me, I guess. Well, I just want him to stop being so shut off to the world. I don't know. I would miss him so much. The way he helps others, thinks about people in need. He gives of himself more than any man I know. He loves God so much. So I don't think he's rude on purpose." Kate looked from Erin to Ivy. "Help?"

Ivy crossed her feet. "Have you talked to him about it? He may be so angry with himself about how he spoke that he is having a hard time speaking to you now. I've learned that I need to speak my mind about how I feel and ask questions before I make assumptions about what others are doing, thinking, or feeling. Often, I learn a new aspect of the person. Sometimes, there is more than I realized." Ivy half shrugged. "When I was in New York, I saw a lot of abuse. That should never be accepted. But arguments happen. And arguments have two sides. So Jonah has his side too."

"I suppose. I know he's busy right now with the giveaway. And then, there is Christmas. I will try to find time to talk to him. If this was just a flirtation or infatuation, I wouldn't care or want to fix things. I really do want to make things right between us." Kate sat up on the bed, glancing between her two friends.

Erin hugged Kate. "The Club is talking to him, too. Maybe things will get worked out. Maybe he feels the same. Let's hope."

SATURDAY, DECEMBER 20,
THE DAY OF THE Christmas Dance

Jonah drove the team out of town. His Santa suit and beard were tucked securely in his sleigh. The toys he and the ladies had made were secured in his basement, ready for the Raven Crest dance tonight. He would force himself to play a jolly Santa and give the Billington children the toys that Josh had made.

A friend, in between towns, had offered the use of his house. There, Jonah donned his Santa suit. A dreary Santa arrived in Billington ready to hear little boys justify their poor behavior and little girls embellish their good behavior and dismiss their naughty.

Jonah played the part as merrily as he could, but he still had a heavy heart. He knew he would have to apologize to Kate. He knew he had hurt her. He was still trying to sort out the mesh of emotions. Why did one woman cause him so much angst?

Returning to Raven Crest, Jonah was just as unsettled as when he left. In the town hall, music played, and couples danced. The tables were laden with cookies, cakes, and pies.

Jonah tried to catch Kate's attention, but she seemed so busy. Worst of all, she seemed fine. She laughed and talked to others, like nothing in the world bothered her, which only added to Jonah's poor mood.

*Does she care at all? Have I messed things up that much? She's more than a woman coming to help. She's Kate, and I want her to be part of my life. But does she want me anymore?*

He caught a signal that his cousin was outside ready to come in. As Jonah walked out of the hall, he noticed Kate standing in a corner, a withdrawn look covering her face. Was she more hurt than she was letting on? Jonah's heart dropped deeper. He was ruining her dance. Would he ever get this girl thing right?

He walked out, and a few minutes later Josh came in with a sack full of toys, ready to spread cheer to little boys and girls.

As planned, Jonah waited about fifteen minutes, just long enough for the children to begin to suspect that Jonah was dressed as Santa. He entered the hall, carrying a plate full of apple slices.

"Does your team like apples?" Jonah flatly asked his cousin.

Josh gave him a concerned look, and then smiled broadly, exclaiming, "Yes, they do!"

Children jumped up and down, pointing at the two men.

"It can't be!"

"I told you he was real!"

Usually, by now, Jonah was stifling a laugh and had to leave. He loved seeing the excitement on the children's faces. However, tonight was different. He gave a weak, quick grin and walked out, waiting for Josh to finish the giveaway.

"Ho, ho, ho, and a merry Christmas to you all." Josh held the town hall door open and waved to the families inside.

Shutting the door and marching to his sleigh, Josh demanded, "What did you do to Miss Goodwin? You both look like someone stole your smiles."

"We argued. I spoke rudely to her. I haven't apologized yet."

"Get on it! She's in there right now about to burst into tears. Fix it!" Josh boarded his sleigh and snapped the team into a trot.

Jonah braced himself against the inevitable. He had to talk to her before he began to procrastinate again.

He crawled up to Kate standing in a corner. "Dance?" he asked, dreading the apology he owed. *Lord, help me to do this right.*

She flatly held out her hand and followed him to the floor.

The warmth of her palm flowed to his shoulder; her other hand rested gently in his. The soft touch sent a jolt through him. His heart beat fast, as he looked into her eyes. He just wanted to hold her, to kiss her and beg for forgiveness. Words were hard; the little he could manage was stolen with one look from her and those beautiful blue eyes. Every thought was driven out of his head, but he knew he needed to say something.

"Sorry about what I said. I'm trying to be more sociable, and you are getting the worst end of it. I was wrong." He held his breath waiting for a response. *That came out easy.*

"Thank you. I'm sorry too. I shouldn't have volunteered you." The song ended. Kate smiled sheepishly.

Jonah took several deep breaths. A pleasant flood rushed through his heart. He kept Kate in his arms. "Another?"

"Please." She stepped just a little closer, eyes locked in his.

Three dances later, Jonah noticed Mama resting, at a table looking tired. "I need to go home. Mama looks beat. I will see you Christmas Eve. I will try it, like you asked."

"Thank you." Kate beamed a broad smile. "I will see you Wednesday."

# CHAPTER 7

# Mistletoe

WEDNESDAY DECEMBER 24,
THE LAYTON'S PARLOR

Jonah kissed his mother's cheek. "Heading to church to help set things up."

"Out again?" Mama set her knitting needles down.

"Aye. It has been a busy week for me. The coffin was a simple pattern, so I finished it in no time then, went to the funeral on Monday. After the funeral, I found a Christmas present for Kate." Jonah grinned.

Mama patted his flushed cheeks. "I enjoy seeing you step out more, and I am thrilled that you patched things up with Miss Goodwin. Enjoy your evening," Mama picked up her needles and began the intricate stitching.

Jonah left home and walked toward the church, feeling the box in his pocket bump his leg. *Oh God, thank You; things are looking up between Kate and me. She will love this present. I need to find a way to get it under the tree without her seeing it. Help me at the church with all the people there. But thank You. I'm not as bad about being with other people as I used to be, especially with Katie nearby.*

He entered the church, with some apprehension, looking around, unsure what to do. Ivy Thompson gave him a job of placing gifts around the tree and making sure everything had a nametag. She gave him a list of presents and whom they were for, just in case something was missing a name.

Kate was busy hanging wreaths and softly humming. Ivy and Erin were setting out candles and hanging mistletoe. Jared walked in and out, putting empty crates away and bringing out more boxes of decorations. A few other people were there, helping make bags of candy. Taylor, an adolescent boy, came in with his guitar and played Christmas carols. Singing and laughter filled the air.

Jonah felt a sense of relief at the tree by himself. Not as many people as he thought were at the church, which helped him relax and enjoy the evening. He whispered Christmas songs and laughed at the Christmas riddles.

"What marks the end of Christmas?" Jared asked the room.

Several answers were given but none was correct.

"No sir-ree. An 's' marks the end of Christmas." Jared slapped his knee, laughing.

Groans and chuckles followed.

"What has many needles but doesn't sew?" Taylor called out.

"A Christmas tree!" Erin answered, "But ours is bare for the gifts."

Kate hung the last wreath. "Then maybe it can sew! I do see a sewing basket under there."

*This is turning out to be a great evening. The only thing to make it better would be a few minutes alone with Katie. A few minutes to get lost in those deep, blue eyes.* The box in his pocket bumped his leg as one last reminder. *After she leaves, I'll put it under the tree, and then I know she won't see or suspect anything.*

Slowly people left the church with good tidings. Erin and Ivy were some of the last stragglers.

"How are you getting home, Kate?" Ivy asked at the door.

"Father is picking me up." Kate straightened a bow on the front pew.

"What about you Erin? Ivy?" Jared shoved the last of the paper in a crate and hoisted it on his hip.

Ivy pulled her coat tighter. "I'm just a few blocks away. I'm walking."

"No you're not!" Erin insisted. "Ben is waiting outside for me. We can give you a ride." She fastened her hood, "This will be such a wonderful time. It's our first Christmas together. After our first Christmas breakfast, we will be here with everyone. I can't wait."

"See you in the morning. Bye Erin, bye Ivy." Kate waved farewell.

Stepping into the middle aisle between the church pews, Kate tilted her head one way and then another. She took a step back and did the same tilt.

*Alone. We are finally alone. Well, Jared is here, but not crowds of people, so we are almost alone. Thank you, God.*

Jonah sauntered his way to Kate and stood next to her, "Something wrong?"

"No, just double- and triple-checking everything," she answered softly.

Jared walked in, picking up another box. "Careful you two." He pointed above them at the mistletoe, then left.

Jonah and Kate looked up at the mistletoe and back to each other. Jonah's heart beat fast, and his breath deepened. He reached over, touching her chin with his knuckle.

"It is tradition," he whispered as he closed his eyes; leaning closer, longing to feel her soft, warm lips on his.

Cold air met his lips, and his hand emptied as she stepped away.

"Tradition isn't a good enough reason anymore," she explained.

Hurt pounded deep in his heart. "Anymore? How many times have you been kissed?"

"A few. How about you?"

He shrugged a noncommittal shrug. Clenching his jaw, he looked away.

"I need to go." She grabbed her coat and ran out the door.

Jonah turned to Jared's office. He needed his friend—and right now. A light tap in his pocket was a grim reminder of the joy he had started with tonight. *Not now. I thought . . . I thought . . . I don't know what I thought . . . but not this.*

Jared shoved more wrapping into a box. The church looked great thanks to the ladies. After the Christmas service tomorrow, he would grab his bag, mount Revelation, and head to his parents' place in Boise. It would take him most of the day to get there but once home, he would spend a few nights with his family and come back Saturday, ready for church on Sunday.

*It could be a tiring trip but worth it. I haven't seen my family in a long while.*

He thought about the small gifts he had bought for his family. He had found a pocketknife at Thompson's for his father. His mother would get a set of lace hankies, and Bella, his sister, would get a small jewelry box.

Was she twelve or thirteen now? Such a large age difference was between them that she barely felt like a sister, more like a close cousin. Mr. Thompson said the jewelry box would work no matter what her age.

Jared turned to Jonah's shuffling footsteps. "What's happened now?"

Jonah sat down without invitation and groaned, "The mistletoe. I tried. She walked away."

"She just left you—hanging there—mid pucker?" Jared asked sympathetically.

"Almost thirty," he said, patting his chest, "Never tried to kiss a girl; never will again. I thought after we danced the other night, I thought there was something special. Guess not." Jonah wiped the corner of his eye with his sleeve.

Jared was stunned. *Thirty and never kissed a girl?*

He remembered his first kiss with fond memories. He had been seventeen. A year or so later he had left for college. Then came the "I'm sorry but—" letter and heartbreak. Other girls had caught his attention but nothing serious. Someday God would bring the right girl along, but who knew when that would be.

"Had calf-love before. Never did nothin' about it." Jonah rubbed his cheek on his shoulder.

"Ah," Jared understood. "Whatcha gonna do now?"

"Go home and batch' it—forever."

Kate ran down the street, emotion clouding her thoughts. She wrapped her arms around herself tightly, trying to keep warm. Paul rode by, making his evening rounds.

"Miss Goodwin! Kate! What's wrong? Do you need help?" He halted Thunder near her.

"No, I need to get to Erin's house, that is all." She looked around, trying to figure out where she was.

"Two blocks to the left. Let me go with you, just in case." Paul eyed her, concerned.

"Thank you." Kate followed Paul, tears clinging to her lashes.

Paul led Thunder, silently walking next to Kate.

In front of the house, Paul tipped his hat. "You have a nice Christmas."

"Thank you. And you, too." Kate forced a smile, and then banged on the front door. "Erin? Erin can I come in?" She waited a moment. "Erin, please. Can I come in? I need to talk to you."

The door opened, and Erin pulled her robe tight around her. "Get in here. It is freezing out there. What happened?"

Erin waved to a figure behind Kate. She glanced over her shoulder to find Paul waiting in the distance. He touched the brim of his hat and left.

Kate dropped onto the sofa. "Jonah happened. What else? Jonah."

Erin sat next to her. "What did he do now?"

"After everyone left—everyone but he and I—oh and Pastor. He tried to kiss me, under some mistletoe. He tried, I almost did, but I didn't. Oh, Erin!" Kate buried her face on Erin's shoulder. "I used to. I have kissed a few men before I accepted Christ. I know I was a flirt back then. I know I didn't make such good choices but now—now I'm trying to be a godly woman."

Erin patted her back. "And you are succeeding. You are a godly woman. What happened then? You didn't let him. Then what?"

"I ran out. I ran here. I didn't know what else to do. Is that how he sees me? Just like those other men did? Getting a few kisses and moving on?"

"I don't think so. That doesn't sound like Jonah. There must be something else."

"I thought I was falling in love. I thought maybe we were falling in love. But love shouldn't hurt me this hard. I always imagined rockets and firecrackers, not this."

"Falling in love is easy. Being in love takes work. Have you prayed about this? Not just telling God what you want but asking Him what He wants?"

Kate shook her head. "I suppose not."

Securing the robe better, Erin reminded Kate, "This could be used as a chance to get closer to God, to learn how to pray for His will not yours."

Nodding, Kate caught a glimpse of the lacy garment underneath Erin's robe. "Oh Erin! You had an evening planned with Ben, didn't you? Why did you let me in? And where is he?"

"He is upstairs. I let you in because I had a friend in need. He understands. And how are you getting home?"

"I hadn't thought that far yet. Father was—"

A loud banging on the door interrupted. "Erin! Do you know where Kate is!" Another bang, "Erin!"

Kate giggled, "I think that is Father now."

Erin left to answer the door. "And I don't think he is very happy."

"Have you seen—Katherine Goodwin, get in that sleigh right now, young lady. I have been looking all over for you!" Father bellowed.

"Yes Father." Kate pecked Erin's cheek. "Merry Christmas."

"Merry Christmas. And remember, he loves you."

"Who?"

"Either one I think. But right now you need to remember your father does."

Kate settled in the sleigh, next to her father. He angrily snapped the team and began to berate Kate for leaving the church with no word. "The only reason I found you so quickly was because I ran into Pa—"

"Father, when did you kiss Mother for the first time?"

"What?" He furrowed his brows. "Why are you asking that?"

"I'm just curious. I know you had a war wedding, but I was just wondering about your courtship."

Father eyed her again. "This March we will be married twenty-seven years. I think I will attempt it then, but it may be too soon."

"Father, really! Honestly, I don't know much about your courtship."

Her father slowed the horses to a steady gait. "We started courting just a few months before the war started. I joined the navy as soon as I heard about Fort Sumter, and we corresponded for about two years. I came home on leave; my mother was not expected to last long. When your mother saw me at the train station, she ran up and gave me a large kiss. I spoke to her father right after that, and the next day we had our wedding at the courthouse. My only regret was my mother. She passed from typhoid the next day. I left again just a few days later, so we say our wedding date is on March 13, but our marriage didn't start until two years later, when the war ended. Why are you so interested?"

"Should a girl kiss before she is engaged?"

"A man of good character shouldn't expect such intimacy until he is ready to make a commitment. That is a man who is worth his salt." The horses stopped at her front door. "Now get your mind off this and get inside. Santa may not be too happy with you right now."

Kate gasped. "Oh, Father!" She rushed into the house and up to her room, crying in her hands. *Oh, Lord help me! I think I love him! Now what?*

### FRIDAY, DECEMBER 26
### BEN AND ERIN'S HOUSE

Jonah leaned to one side, trying to avoid Erin's brisk reach over his shoulder. She set the plate of roast beef on the table with a thump. Her lips pursed in a grimace, scowling at Jonah. He looked around the table hoping someone would explain Erin's gruffness.

The bowl of mashed potatoes was next to be plunked down. A smattering of potatoes fell from the bowl onto the table.

"Excuse me," she growled through clenched teeth, reaching passed Jonah to clean up the mess.

The men looked at Jonah. Ben silently asked, "What did you do?"

Jonah turned palms up to indicate that he was just as lost as they were.

"Erin, honey," Ben started tentatively. "Is something wrong?"

"Ask Jonah," Erin said firmly.

Jonah gaped. "What did I do?"

"You hurt my friend. Do you know how many times Kate has cried over you?" Erin tapped her foot, glaring at Jonah.

"She's the one that . . ." He looked away unable to recount what happened on Christmas Eve.

"What? She's the one who didn't kiss you?" Erin stood with her hands on her hips, staring narrow eyed at Jonah. "Why should she? One day you're telling her to be quiet and the next, you're trying to kiss her!"

Ben, Paul, and Corbin stared at Jonah in surprise.

Jonah dropped his head in his hands. Looking back at Erin, he begged for help. "We made up at the dance. I thought we were good. I thought we had an understanding. What do I do now? I—I—I think I'm in love with her."

"Figure out if you are or aren't. I can't help you until you know for sure." Scowling, she folded her arms in front of her.

Jonah ran his hands over his mouth and through his beard, and then he rubbed his forehead. "I do. I love her," he admitted. "I just don't know how to tell her. I've never done this before. And I've messed things up so badly. Everything I do seems wrong."

"Then tell her that," Erin instructed, a softer tone ebbing into her voice. "That's all she wants to hear."

He nodded, feeling defeated. "First thing in the morning," he procrastinated.

Erin reached for his plate, pulling it away from him. "No! Now!"

Jonah glanced around the table, trying to find support. He was met with shrugs and points to the door. "Paul? You think I should wait don't you? Cards tonight, right? Maybe I should wait until Jared gets back. Then I could talk to a pastor first, right?" *Please Paul, you're my last chance. I don't know what to say to her.*

Paul shook his head. "Might as well get this over with."

Slowly, Jonah walked to the door, donning his coat and hat with one last look backward. Everyone watched with heartfelt sympathy. Jonah was walking into the unknown, and he had to do it alone.

Jonah sulked home, dreading the inevitable. He saddled Salt and rode to the mayor's house across town. Snow lightly fell from the night sky; his breath left a foggy trail behind him. *God, what do I say? How do I explain why I'm so bad at this? I can't find the words. I just want her to feel my heart.*

Knocking on the Goodwins' front door, he was still undecided. He would have to open up, let her in his heart, and hope she accepted him. But how? What words would he use?

Kate answered his knock, shocked to see him. A sense of hurt was mingled with surprise and Jonah knew that hurt belonged to him.

"None," Jonah said.

Confusion replaced Kate's surprise. "What?" She began to back way just a little, like she might close the door.

"On Christmas Eve, you asked how many girls I had kissed before. None. Not like that."

Kate reached for her coat, which was hanging by the door.

On the porch, Kate leaned against the rail. Jonah clumsily searched for words, looking at anything but her.

Pulling her coat tighter, Kate admitted, "Before I accepted Christ, I kissed a few gentlemen. But now I won't; not unless there is an understanding. When you tried to kiss me, I thought you expected me to be that kind of girl again. I thought we had worked out our argument—at least most of it."

"No, I didn't expect that. I just wanted things to be right between us. I just wanted you to know how sorry I was and how much I miss you; how much I want to court you. But I did it wrong. I was wrong again."

"And then you didn't come on Christmas morning to the church. I thought . . ."

Jonah shook his head. "Esther and her husband, Bob, showed up on Christmas Eve, with their children, right about the time I got home. Mama asked if we could spend Christmas morning at home as a family." He fumbled in his pocket, feeling the gift he had planned to give her on Christmas. "I bought this for you." He held out a small black box.

Kate opened it, inside was a silver hair barrette, with a sapphire stone in the middle. It would look perfect with almost anything she wore.

"Thank you. It's pretty," she said quietly.

"Not as pretty as you, Katie Cat. I mean Kate."

She smiled sweetly. "I like Katie Cat . . . from you. I want things to be right between us, too. I want to be close to you."

He took the barrette out of the box and fastened it in her hair. Jonah stroked her cheek softly, gazing into her deep blue eyes. "If I were to try and kiss you again, would you walk away?"

She pressed in close, shook her head slowly, and lifted her chin, her eyes gently closing.

Jonah leaned down, cupping the back of her head. Carefully, he pressed his lips to hers. He pulled away slightly and rubbed his nose against her nose. Then came back for a fuller, deeper kiss.

"I need to talk to your father about courting you," he whispered, barely leaving her lips.

Kate murmured, "He's inside," and pulled him closer, unwilling to leave his arms.

In his hold, she shivered a little, and Jonah insisted they go in. Cupping her hand in his, he walked in the house with her. Mayor Goodwin was in his office, going through a new town proposal. Jonah knocked on the open door with Kate's hand still in his.

Mayor Goodwin arched his brows and cleared his throat. "Excuse me?"

"Can we talk?" Jonah asked. *Can he tell how much I care about her? How much I love her? Did I tell her that I love her? I don't think I did. I will soon.*

Mr. Goodwin exhaled deeply. "I knew this day would come sooner than I expected. Kate, please leave so the men can talk."

Kate squeezed Jonah's hand and gave her father a warning look, as she left for the parlor, where her mother chatted with anyone in earshot.

Jonah closed the door and nervously brushed his hands against the leg of his pants. "I'd like to court Kate," he spat out.

"Court?" Mr. Goodwin clarified.

"Court for a respectable amount of time. Then . . . marry?"

Mayor Goodwin inhaled and exhaled several times. "Speak to me again when the 'respectable amount of time' is done. But courting is granted . . . for now," he warned.

"Thanks!" Jonah spun around, "I've got to tell Katie." He rushed out, swung Kate around and kissed her. *Will I ever get tired of that?*

Mrs. Goodwin pulled Mayor close to her and loudly whispered, "It looks like our baby is growing up."

Jonah released Kate, his cheeks reddening, "Ummm . . . Mrs. Goodwin . . . ummm . . ."

"No need to explain. I understand." Mrs. Goodwin wrapped her arm around the mayor's waist.

"Can you come back to The Club with me? Everyone will want to know." Jonah slapped his forehead. "I rode Salt. No sleigh."

Kate gently squeezed his hand. "Then I will ride Princess. I can't wait to tell Erin everything."

# CHAPTER 8

# Too Much

Kate urged Princess to Jonah's house Saturday, ready to start their social planning. Her list of dates filled the handbag on her arm. A brisk breeze stung her cheeks, creating a rosy glow.

Tethering Princess to the front hitching post, Kate began to wonder. *Will he be resistant?* She mounted the steps and squared her shoulders. *No! All I need is a winning smile and a few kisses.* The smile appeared immediately. *That will help pull that turtle out of his shell. He may resist a little at first, but soon he will see all the fun he is missing. Besides, I have been praying,* she concluded triumphantly, knocking on the Layton's' front door.

Jonah answered the door with a roughish grin. She wrapped her arms around him and snuggled close with a coy, "Missed you."

"Missed you, too." He leaned down to punctuate his sentiments with a kiss.

Mrs. Layton politely cleared her throat, interrupting the kiss and reminding them of her presence.

Kate smiled sheepishly, casting a glance at Jonah, silently telling him she wanted to continue their interlude later. "Do you have an 1891 calendar, Mrs. Layton?"

"Oh, I just got one yesterday. Do you need it?"

Kate nodded and led Jonah to the kitchen. "Lots to do; we need to write these things down, so you don't forget." She flashed her best smile at Jonah. "Planning our social life together will take some time." Sitting at the table, Kate started pointing out dates. "This week, on the thirty-first, is a New Year's Eve party at the Clayborns'." She scanned the month of January. Pointing to another date, "Right here is a dinner party at Judge Ashburn's."

Jonah watched with a wrinkled brow.

"Oh, and a vaudeville show is right here. Vaudeville is a new type of show and becoming quite the rage. I just ordered the tickets." Kate beamed a brilliant smile. Noticing his look of horror, she assured him, "You will like it, it is supposed to be funny."

Her heart dropped in disappointment as his scowl deepened. Kate mustered up her resolve and looked around, in a hopeless attempt to locate a pen and ink.

"Is there something to write with?" She held her empty hand out, expecting a writing utensil to appear. "And don't you have a small book to keep track of this? It's usually in your jacket pocket."

"I can't go to all that." He waved at the calendar. "And I heard about that show. It's for Friday night. You know I have the Club then."

"I can exchange them for Saturday night. Friday night is here in Raven Crest, but Saturday is in Billington. Maybe Erin and Ben will come with us," she added, hoping the other couple would help convince him.

"Can't we just stay home and enjoy the quiet?" he implored.

"It won't be that bad. I'll be there with you." She flashed a bright smile, trying to melt his heart.

Kate started talking about events in February. Jonah stretched back, folded his arms, fixing a stare at the wall. Kate mentioned a few more dates, doubtfully taken aback at his cold stature. She looked at the calendar and back at him.

*Maybe I'm expecting too much too soon. The New Year's Eve party at the Clayborns' promises to be a wonderful evening. I should start there and go slow.*

Kate returned the calendar to its spot on a shelf, and then kissed Jonah's cheek. "Maybe we can finish this later."

Jonah shrugged, turning his face up for a better kiss. That seemed to help, but he still appeared stubborn about the parties. Kate left a little deflated but just as determined as before to pull him out of that shell.

New Year's Eve
The Layton house

Jonah pulled his heavy coat on. "I'm leaving Mama. Are you sure you don't want to come?"

"No thank you, dear. I just can't stay up that late any more. Go and have a good time with Kate. And remember, you are not that timid little boy anymore."

In the stables, he hitched the team to the sleigh and drove to the Goodwins' house. *Lord, help me. I have to get through tonight, and this next week is already full. I get tired just planning all this stuff. But I don't want to disappoint Kate.*

Slowly he mounted the steps, dreading the rest of the evening. He knocked on the front door and waited impatiently.

Mr. Goodwin opened the door, letting Jonah in.

"Is Kate ready?" He asked trying to hide the annoyance.

A movement at the top of the stairs grabbed his attention.

Kate descended slowly. She was dressed beautifully. The silver-blue gown sparkled with every movement. Her hair was pulled up in the latest fashion, but the light shining in her eyes was what melted Jonah's heart.

All thoughts left his mind. He was captured by her sparkling smile and gaze.

At the foot of the steps, Kate glanced at the coat rack. "I may need my wrap," she softly reminded him.

He grappled for the wrap, refusing to take his eyes off her. Soon, he found it and wrapped a thick cloak around her shoulders. Jonah froze with his arms partially encircling Kate and inhaled the sweet scent of perfume. He pulled her just a little closer and inhaled again captivated by her presence.

She softly stroked his hand that was still holding her cape.

His heart soared at her winning smile and gentle touch. "Ummm . . . the . . . ummm . . . The Clayborns' is only a bit away . . . ummm" Jonah's heart pounded hard. He gulped, trying to regain his self-composer. "Mr. Goodwin, are you coming?"

Mayor chuckled. "We will be there shortly. Just waiting for Mrs. Goodwin."

Jonah nodded awkwardly and escorted Kate to the sleigh. He carefully tucked the lap blanket around her. "This should help keep you warm until we get inside."

The team was snapped into a trot. The Clayborns' house was just a few blocks away from the Goodwins' house. A stable boy offered to stable the team during the party.

Inside, a band played on the third floor. Flickering candlelights glistened off the silver candelabras. An elaborately decorated Christmas tree graced one corner of the ballroom and evergreen boughs were hung throughout. People filled the house, wandering in and out of different rooms but most of the guests lingered near the dance floor. Serving staff wandered the house offering small delights and glasses of wine.

Jared mingled with a group of men, discussing upcoming town meetings. Ben and Erin floated from room to room, talking, dancing, and enjoying the evening.

Jonah tried to be more sociable for Kate's sake. He followed her around, forcing a smile and feeling more and more drained. As soon as he could, he asked Kate to dance with him. There, on the dance floor, he found himself lost in her arms. The music carried them to another place, a place of just them, no one else. Then the song ended, and Kate pulled him to the crowds, laughing and talking to everyone.

"When can we go, Katie Cat?" Fatigue banged at the back of Jonah's head.

"We have to stay until midnight. Why are you in such a hurry? The toy giveaway is done. You can rest from all that until next year."

Jonah rubbed the back of his neck. "I still have other things I need to do. The first chamber of commerce meeting is in a few days. And Doc told me that Old Mr. Zuckerman isn't doing well. I may be needed there sometime this week. I will try to stay a little longer."

Kate pulled him into a quiet hallway and kissed him. "Thank you. It will be midnight in a few minutes. Maybe one more dance until then?"

"I'd like that." He leaned down for a better kiss.

Instead, Kate dragged him to the dance floor and lined them up for a reel. One dance turned into four until the music stopped and guests gathered around Mr. Clayborn. Champagne was offered to toast the New Year. Jonah refused as politely as he could.

"Oh, you must! It is a tradition." Mrs. Clayborn thrust a glass in his hand and pushed her way to the front.

"Kate, I can't drink this." Jonah looked for a table to set the glass on.

"Just hold it for now, please," Kate begged. "It is some of the best there is."

The clock struck midnight, and the guests cheered, toasting the New Year. Jonah handed his glass to a man walking around with a tray of drinks.

"Katie Cat, I have to leave. If you want to stay longer, I will ask Ben or your father to give you a ride home. But I need to go now, please."

Kate glanced around the room. "I will go with you. I just need one last look at everything. It is so beautiful."

In the sleigh, Kate cuddled under the thick lap blanket. "Why won't you have a drink? It's not against the Bible. You wouldn't even have a swallow."

"Do you know how Papa died?"

"A hunting accident, wasn't it? What does that have to do with a New Year's Eve toast?"

Jonah inhaled trying to control the sting of tears. "We were hunting. I was about twenty. It was my first trip with him and a small group of men. Your father was there, too. I felt so grown up.

"A group of men at another camp site started drinking. The night carried on, and they got louder and more drunk. They started firing their guns at the sky. Papa was trying to get me in my tent for protection. He thought if I was in the tent, lying down, then I wouldn't get hurt. I argued with him. There was a loud bang of gunfire. The next thing I knew, there was blood on my face and Papa was on the ground. He was shot in the head right in front of me. If I had gone in like he said, then he would still be alive. I won't touch guns or drink. When Mrs. Clayborn kept pushing it on me, I knew I had to leave." He blinked back a few tears. "I've never told anyone that whole thing before."

Jonah wiped the drops that trailed down his cheeks. *Those words came out easy. They just seemed to flow. I can talk to Kate better than anyone.*

Kate sniffled. "Father never told me all that. I remember he used to hunt, often with your father, I think. Then he stopped hunting all of a sudden. He will have a glass of wine at dinner or after-dinner brandy, but not both. He is very careful. And he doesn't talk about your father much. When he does, he gets . . . well, I don't know; just not himself. Now I understand why. I didn't know all the details. I'm sorry that happened." She snuggled closer. "I will be more aware of such things from now on."

Jonah leaned his head against her. "Thank you, my Katie Cat."

## Wednesday, January 3, 1891
## Raven Crest Town Hall

"If we all do it, then those good-for-nothings will leave. And we can have our town the way it should be." Mr. Wilson, the town tailor bellowed his opinion to the men who had met to form a new chamber of commerce.

"Those people aren't good-for-nothings. Many of them work in our homes. Just because their color is dark doesn't mean we treat them poorly." Mayor Goodwin slammed his fist on the table. "The purpose of this meeting is to create an organization that will help improve Raven Crest for business."

Mr. Wilson folded his arms. "Getting rid of those people will improve business."

A small mummer rustled through the town hall. The room was divided. Half agreed with all businesses having clear black code signs; the other side was opposed to the signs anywhere.

Jonah rocked his chair back until it leaned against the wall. *I'm so tired, God. This was supposed to be a friendly business meeting. And Wilson is using it to push his hatred of all black people. Maybe it's time for me to leave.*

He nudged Corbin and nodded to the door. "I'm out of here."

Corbin agreed, "Not what I was expecting at all."

Jonah and Corbin quietly stood and headed for the door. Jonah wanted to leave as inconspicuously as he could.

"And where do you two think you are going? The first cowards to leave, huh?" Mr. Wilson called loudly.

Turning slowly, Jonah glared at the man demanding the crowd's attention. His long legs stretched the length of the town hall to Mr. Wilson. Jonah straightened up to his full height, towering over the other man. "I came here to talk business not opinion. If you want to post one of those signs, you can. I refuse to. I also refuse to be part of an organization that tells me how to run my business." He faced the men in the hall. "Anyone else brave enough to stand up to this man and his foolish ideas?" He marched to the door.

"When you are ready to discuss a chamber like we planned, let me know. To me, this sounds more like a—" He turned to face Mr. Wilson, "What do you call it 'the ghosts of the dead confederates' meeting."

Jonah stomped to the door, slammed it behind him, and marched home.

Corbin rushed next to him. "I'm proud of you. Never heard you talk so much or so firmly."

"I'm learning. I just can't be a part of that meeting. Not the way it was going."

"You look exhausted. What's wrong?"

Jonah dropped on his front porch bench. "Party at the Clayborns' last week. Yesterday, I was across the river because a mama died giving birth. I know Mr. Zuckerman won't make it much longer—the old one, not the young one. Kate wants me to go to the Ashburns' for another party. And she ordered tickets for a vaudeville show on Saturday. Now, that meeting. I feel like nothing is left of me."

"Get to bed. You need some rest. That would be a full schedule for anyone. If I hear about a real chamber meeting, I'll let you know."

"Thanks." Jonah dragged himself inside his house, and up to his room. He fell face down on his bed, his toes hanging over the end. Drifting off to sleep, his thoughts began to wander, *I need a bigger bed. This one is too short for me; it has been for a while. I'll tell Mama in the morning.*

SATURDAY NIGHT

"Thanks for coming Ben and Erin. And thanks for taking your team. I'm too beat." Jonah rested his head against the back of the sleigh. His fingers laced with Kate's, under the lap blanket.

"I heard that meeting was a bust. What happened? Why are you so tired?" Ben waved to a passing family.

"Wilson's from the south. He wants Idaho to be just like those states or as white as possible. I left. I don't know if there will be another meeting or not. Zuckerman finally passed on the other day. His poor family took care of him for years. The last few weeks were awful; he was so weak and helpless."

Kate rubbed her shoulder against his. "Now, you have a wonderful evening full of laughter and songs. You can just relax and enjoy."

Jonah smiled weakly. *I just want to be home. To be home with no one expecting anything from me. No parties, no meetings, no coffins to build, just home and quiet.*

Squeezing his hand tighter, Kate leaned against his shoulder. This helped some, but what about inside? He can't touch her in public; that would be improper for a courting couple.

In Billington's small theater, Ben found the four seats at the end of the row. Jonah sat on the very edge, so Kate was the only one next to him. He rested his arm next to Kate's and wrapped one of his fingers around hers. When he was sure no one could see the affectionate touch, he closed his eyes, and stiffened, trying to make it through the night.

The show began with boisterous applause. Jonah stiffened at the noise and anxiously looked around. *It's just clapping not gunfire. Just relax.*

Jonah closed his eyes again and tried to enjoy the show. He tapped his foot to the music and smiled at the jokes. But he couldn't relax, not the way Kate wanted him to. He was enduring this for her. He wouldn't be able to loosen up until he was out of the crowd and in his own home.

Ben tapped his hand and motioned toward the stage. "We're leaving."

A group of men were on the stage in blackface, making crude, racial jokes.

Jonah looked at Kate. "I can't stay for this."

Kate gave a disappointed frown and gathered her things.

The four went to a nearby café for a bite to eat and discuss the evening.

Erin started. "I can't watch those shows. You all know I don't know my mother's parents." She looked around the table. There were nods and questioning looks. "After the War, my mother was disowned by her parents. They found out she had helped the Underground Railroad a few times. That was enough for her parents. Even though she was married, they were furious that she would take such a risk. They won't speak to her to this day."

She looked down trying to control the threatening tears.

Ben gently pulled her head to his shoulder, and then shared his experience. "I went to college back east. One of the students was black, and he was probably the smartest fella there. When the students were called upon to argue cases for practice, he could out argue many of the professors. He was treated horribly because of his color. Some professors refused to give him the marks he earned; some students jeered and made fun of him." He looked down in shame. "I didn't join in, but I didn't try to stop it, either. That was just as bad as doing it myself." He shrugged, "Now, I try to take a stand however I can, like walking out of a show."

Jonah picked at the food on his plate. "When I go across the river, to the black community, I see hurt there, just like when I'm needed in town. We are all made in God's image, and He died for all of us. When any of His children are hurt, I think God hurts too. I can't be a part of hurting His children."

Kate rubbed Jonah's hand. "I had not seen an act like that. I wanted to see the act before I made a decision about it. But now I see how crude it is." She looked puzzled. "I know I don't have much experience with that race, other than house help and such. But I don't understand the jokes. It's not like the people I know at all."

Jonah gazed at the beautiful woman next to him. His heart melted for her. His hope rose. *Maybe she's seeing things my way. Seeing that we don't need to spend all our time at parities and such. Maybe she can see how nice a quiet evening at home is.*

Erin explained another situation she was going through with a tenant. "After the commerce meeting, I've noticed some signs up in windows. I try not to go into those establishments. The baker that rents one of my businesses has a 'black in back' sign, so he doesn't allow anyone of color to enter his front door. If they want service, even if it's for their employer, they must come around to the back and wait for him to finish with his white customers. Then he will help them. I've carefully read the rental agreement. And I can't tell him how to run his business."

Ben held Erin's hand. "There's no law against such things. All we can do is pray for him and for us. We're praying his attitude changes, but we are also praying that we can be good witnesses; that God brings something along to help him see people for who they really are—God's children."

The ride home was quiet. In the wagon, Jonah leaned against the back of the seat and wrapped his hand around Kate's. Slowly the tension from the last few days drifted away. Kate snuggled closer, resting her head against his shoulder. Jonah scooted over as close as he could. *Thank You, God. This is better than I ever imagined. I could spend the rest of my life right here next to Kate.*

# CHAPTER 9

# Love Seeketh Not Her Own

FEBRUARY 6

BEN AND ERIN'S HOUSE

Friday night, Jonah sulked in a corner, stirring his coffee. *Lord, help me. I'm exhausted,* he moaned silently.

Kate and Erin cleared the dinner dishes and talked. They talked about the weather, spring-cleaning and upcoming events. Spring activities were the main focus of conversation. There seemed to be no end to their constant chatter.

Erin stored the last of the cleaned dishes and announced, "We are going to Ivy's. The Ladies Auxiliary meets in a few weeks to plan some spring frolics for the children and the town. We want to get a good jump on it."

The chatter faded as they left the house. Jonah dropped his head and exhaled his weariness.

Jared poured some cream into his cup of coffee. "I heard you had to go to Billington for your services. How many times have you been there?"

"Two since the New Year. Once across the river, and once for Mr. Zuckerman. Plus the Smiths' right before Christmas."

"So you need something better to think about. How's it going with Kate?" Jared asked.

Jonah glared at him.

"You got your girl. Shouldn't there be a smile on your face?" Jared questioned, shuffling the cards.

"We gotta say last week's verse first." Paul reminded gruffly.

Each man took his turn quoting the Bible verse, then Jared dealt the cards and named the game.

Ben anted up. "Jonah, what happened? Things sound good from where I stand."

"I have her, but I don't know for how long," Jonah replied flatly.

Ben and Jared looked at him confused. Paul became intent on his cards, and Corbin shifted uneasily in his seat.

"Kate likes parties and social gatherings with crowds. I'm better than I used to be with crowds, but I still don't like them. And I am getting busier than ever between here, across the river, and Billington. The chamber of commerce is drawing more of my attention. There has been two meetings since that first one. Now we're talking about how to run elections for positions and what to expect from the meetings. It's hard trying to do it all. I feel like I have nothing left to give."

"Have you talked to her? Have you told her how drained you feel? Maybe you can make compromises, only go out a few times a month," Jared suggested.

"I'll try." Jonah shrugged; doubtful that anything would help.

"What have you done for her lately?" Ben inquired.

Jonah was taken back. "Everything we do is what she wants and plans. It's all about her."

Ben shook his head. "When is the last time *you* did something for her. Just to put a smile on her face?" He motioned around the room. "I hate flowers inside."

The other men chuckled, noticing the flowers throughout the room.

"They drop petals and leaves. They are so messy, and you know how I am about messes." The men nodded and groaned their understanding. "But Erin loves flowers. She has that hot house so she can grow them in the winter. It used to get me so mad to come home and find dirty water in vases, petals, and flowers over . . . everything.

"Then, I picked some for her because she was having a difficult day. That's when I realized, I love that smile. I love that smile more than I hate those flowers. Sometimes I pick her flowers just to see her smile. Have you done anything like that? Just to make her smile?"

Jonah thought about it. *I love Kate's smile. I love seeing the gleam in her eyes when she is happy or surprised by something. I've been so concerned about how I feel and what she's making me do that I haven't been thinking of her, only me.*

Jared reminded him of 1 Corinthians 13, the love chapter. "Remember, it tells us how we should show love not what someone else should do for us. Try reading it and look at it from her eyes. Will she say you're following it?"

"One of the hardest lessons I had to learn was to think about Erin and how I was treating her. It's not just about me and what I want." Ben smiled sheepishly. "Still working on that one. Kate might understand better if you talked to her about it. Maybe on Valentine's Day. You could do something special for her and share how you feel."

The Club played quietly for a few hours until Corbin won that night's chips. He somberly gathered the pile toward him.

"I've been thinking about leaving the Club," he confessed.

Jared, Ben, and Jonah were shocked. Paul studied the table, tracing a pattern in the wood.

"I'm not leaving. It's just been about girls so much lately. First Erin, and now Kate. What you said tonight," Corbin looked at Ben, "it's not always about you, made me realize the Club isn't always about me." Corbin nudged Paul next to him. "Paul, I think we both need this. Our verse this week is a familiar one, but I need a refresher. Galatians 6:2. 'Bear ye one another's burdens and so fulfill the law of Christ.' I know it's not what I had picked out when we started, but it's what I need tonight. Besides, someday I may need your help with a girl." Corbin gave a snort of a laugh, "Not that any are on the horizon."

Jonah wrote down the Bible verse in a leather bound notebook he usually brought to the poker game. He tugged on his jacket and trudged home. *Ben said he'd give Kate a ride to her house so I could go straight home and think. Think and pray. Lord, help me.* The verse about Christ's yoke being light filtered through Jonah's mind. He dropped into bed and begged for the lighter yoke. Wrapped in his Father's arms, Jonah drifted into a deep sleep.

That night in bed, Erin lay in Ben's arms. He explained what had happened at the table earlier.

"We had a similar conversation," Erin shared. "But I used peas as my example not flowers."

"I should have known you would have guessed the flowers. And knowing how much you hate peas but make them just for me, makes them taste that much better." Ben laughed.

Tilting his head down, Ben kissed her. "I love you so much."

Erin rolled over with her back to Ben. "I can't," she said flatly.

Ben pulled her gently toward him. "I know. I understand what's happening. Just because I kiss you doesn't mean I want . . . more."

He had seen the rags in the outhouse bucket that afternoon when he came home. Ben knew what that meant. He also knew Erin's moods would become erratic right before and during this time. The depression seemed to get worse each month.

"I was hoping by now I would have a secret I was trying to keep from you but failing," she admitted sadly.

"We've only been married a few months. It takes time. Some couples are married for a year or more before . . . booties are being knitted," he smiled. *Is that why she gets so moody? Is starting a family that important to her?*

She nuzzled into his chest. "I guess I'm being impatient."

"When it happens, I will be thrilled. Until then, we get more nights like this." He held her close.

*I'm in no hurry. I love these nights. But a baby seems to be the most important thing to her right now. God, help me. I need to know what You want for us. And what I need to do for her.*

SATURDAY, FEBRUARY 14
THE LAYTON HOUSE

"Keep your eyes closed." Jonah covered Kate's eyes with his hand. "There are two steps here. Careful."

"I can't see a thing. I promise I will only look at the steps. I just don't want to trip." Kate heart was about to burst. *What does he have planned? He said dinner tonight; now it looks like more than that. But we are at his house. I'm so confused.*

"All right, just peek down at the steps, so you don't trip. We are at my house for dinner. Mama is here, so we aren't alone. But I think you will like it."

He carefully led her into the kitchen and uncovered her eyes. "Now you can look."

Kate gasped in surprise. A beautiful hand-stitched tablecloth covered the table, along with Mrs. Layton's best China. A large bouquet of flowers rested at one end and two candles flickered in the middle.

"This is so wonderful. How beautiful."

"Mama made veal for dinner. She found a recipe for a French soup. I thought you might like it." He handed her a Valentine's card. "Sommers, at the print shop, says these are spreading like wildfire." A small blush flushed his cheeks. "Will you be my Valentine?"

Kate threw her arms around his neck. "Always. Thank you so much." *He did all this for me? I am the luckiest girl in the world.*

Jonah pulled her chair out from the table corner. She took the offered seat beaming a smile at Jonah. He sat at the head of the table next to Kate, his knee brushing against her knee.

Mrs. Layton stood at the stove stirring a pot of soup. "This soup is done. I'll pull the veal out now. Then I will be in the parlor, if you need anything. The cake is on the counter. Enjoy your meal."

Kate rose, ready to prepare the plates. Jonah rested his hand on her shoulder. "No, I fix the plates. You sit and enjoy."

Jonah poured a bowl of soup and set it in front of Kate. Jonah went back to the stove to prepare the dinner plates. Each plate was piled with veal, rice, green beans, and a dinner roll. Jonah sat one plate in front of Kate next to the bowl of soup. Her eyes widened at the amount of food.

"You don't have to eat it all. It's probably too much. I asked her to make a velvet cake. That's my favorite, and I didn't know what yours was." Jonah bowed his head and blessed the food.

Kate sipped the soup. "Mmmm, this is delicious. The soup does remind me of Paris. And I love velvet cakes. But I admit, now that I am learning how to bake cakes, the simpler angel food cakes are becoming my favorite."

She held out her spoon. "You haven't tried it yet."

He accepted the offered bite, capturing her in his gaze.

"I didn't think you would do anything about today, considering how much you hate social activities." Kate looked away, astonished at how much the truth hurt.

Jonah forced her eyes back to him with a gentle brush of her cheek. "Katie Cat, This . . ." He motioned around the room. "I enjoy this. No crowds, no loud noises. Just us together . . . alone. I wish I could be a man who enjoyed parties and things the way you like them, but I'm not that man. I'm trying. It just . . ." This time he looked away.

"Tell me. I want to understand. I want to help." Kate rested her hand on his knee.

"It just takes so much out of me. After going to parties and such, then I have to help those in need. Now the chamber is having regular meetings. I have been elected as one of the board members. I don't have to talk or anything, but because I stood up to Wilson at the first meeting, everyone wants me to help lead." He shook his head trying to clear his thoughts. "Anyway. I just need time at home being quiet, resting. I use that time to pray, read my Bible, seek God for areas I need to grow in and just rest. But I haven't had that lately; we go out so much. Then, I have things for work and the town. I'm exhausted when I get home. I feel like nothing is left of me."

"I had no idea. I'm so sorry. I didn't mean to do that to you. I just wanted to spend time with you. Maybe we could work out a compromise. I will only pick two social engagements a month. We can agree on how long we will be there. But please tell me if I start asking more of you again."

Jonah fed her a bite of veal. "I will and thank you for understanding. Please let me know if you need more. You can go without me, or I will try to do more."

She leaned over and offered a kiss. "After we finish here, you can show me what a quiet evening at home is like. Your mother is here, so we don't have to concern ourselves about looking proper."

Kate gazed dreamily into Jonah's eyes, taken by the handsome man in front of her. She offered him bites of veal and accepted bites from him. *I don't see that awkward little turtle anymore. I see a strong man of character. A man who loves God, and whom I love.* She sighed at the thought. *Yes, I love him.*

"Are you ready for a piece of cake?" He stroked her hair. "And can we share it? I am enjoying this."

"Yes, please. Would you like me to serve?"

"No. This is your night. I take care of you." Jonah left the table and cut a piece of cake.

Kate was captured in his eyes again as they fed each other. The cake was gone before either one wanted the evening to end.

"Can we go to the parlor with your mother?" Kate took a stack of dishes to the sink.

"Of course. I can whittle; Mama is probably knitting. What would you like to do?"

"Can I read a story out loud? Who is your favorite author?"

Jonah chuckled. "Edgar Allen Poe, but I don't think you would like those stories. Mama may have something from Elizabeth Browning or Shakespeare."

"Maybe we can find something we will both like. I will look; maybe you have *Robin Hood* in the library." *This is wonderful, we are never this quiet at home.*

Jonah led Kate to the parlor. She thumbed through the shelves of books and picked out *Ivanhoe*. Kate settled on the sofa. Jonah leaned back next to her and stretched his legs.

"Whittling can wait 'til tomorrow. If I start to snore, I'm sorry. This is just so relaxing."

Kate giggled. "And I will only kick you if you snore loudly. Shall I begin?"

Settling on the sofa, Kate realized, *I could spend every night like this. Well, almost every night. Thank You, God for showing me his heart.*

Softly, Kate began to read. In a few minutes a light snore rumbled from Jonah.

Mrs. Layton stifled a laugh. "He could scare a bear with that noise."

Kate marked the place she left off and gently nudged Jonah's foot. He jumped with a start.

"How loud?" Jonah rubbed the sleep from his eyes.

"Loud enough for me to know it's time to go home." Kate grinned and rubbed his knee.

Jonah stretched. "Yes, but it will be a good night's sleep when I get back. This has been a . . ." He stretched again with a large yawn.

"Yes, it has been a wonderful night." Kate wrapped her cloak around her. *And I know what I will dream about tonight.*

# CHAPTER 10

# A Beautiful Spring Night

MARCH 1

THE GOODWIN HOUSE

Kate bounced down the stairs and then curled up on the sofa in the parlor. "Ouch! These rags are so tight." Kate rubbed her sore head. "Meridith will be staying at her parents' house tonight, so she ragged my hair earlier than usual. Now I get to spend the rest of the evening looking like this." She waved her hand over her head. "And you get to look at it all through dinner."

Father chuckled, "Oh, the price women pay for such beauty."

Pondering the pervious few weeks, Kate settled deeper into the sofa. *At least Jonah doesn't see this. Hmmm . . . Jonah . . .* her heart flipped slightly, thinking of him and that wonderful Valentine's dinner. *What could I do for him? We've only gone to poker nights, and I have two events planned for March, but is there something I can do for him? To make him happy?*

A knock at the front door stirred Kate from her thoughts. Mother answered the door and led Jonah to the parlor, calling out, "Kate dear, you have company."

Kate jumped up, covering her head with a muffled scream. "No! Jonah! Not like this! Don't look at me, please!"

Stifling a laugh, Jonah turned his back. Over his shoulder, he held up two tickets. "For an opera. Next Saturday night."

"An opera? But . . . oh, how could you?" Kate fumbled for anything to cover her head. She located a blanket on the sofa and draped it over her head and onto her shoulders.

"Thank you so much," she stammered, near tears.

"Can I turn around, please?" Jonah glanced over his shoulder expectantly.

"Yes, I suppose." Kate fixed her embarrassment toward the floor.

Jonah stroked her cheek. "I often wondered how you got such perfect curls. And all I wanted was to see you smile, not cry."

"Really?" A smile beamed through her tears. "Thank you so much."

Looking to Father, Jonah waved the tickets a little. "Sir, it's in Billington. Ben is taking Erin, so we can all ride together."

Father slowly nodded, with a look of warning.

"But I already picked the two events we would go to this month. Should I cancel one of them?" Kate asked.

"No. This is something extra for you. Gotta go. Heading home from across the river," he explained.

Kate followed him outside and kissed him deeply. She wanted him to know how much she appreciated the tickets.

"I love you and your kisses, but please don't feel like you . . . owe me." Jonah said hesitantly.

"You love me?" Kate asked timidly.

Jonah tilted her chin up, looking in her eyes. "Yes, I love you."

She whispered, wide-eyed, "I love you, too."

Kate floated into the house. Tossing the blanket on the sofa, she sighed. *He loves me. Me . . . even with rags in my hair, he loves me!*

"Can we eat dinner now? I'm starving?" Father held open the dining room door.

At the dining table, Mother had to call for her attention. "Kate. Kate, dear. Kate! The Ladies Auxiliary will be planning a spring dance, maybe a picnic. Do you think you could help?"

Kate dreamily responded, "Whatever you think Mother." *He loves me!*

SATURDAY EVENING, MARCH 14

Kate and Erin talked about the coming dance as Ben drove the new, larger buggy to Billington. Jonah sat silently in the back of the buggy next to Kate.

The weather was nice and fresh on the beautiful, spring evening. A cool breeze fluttered through the air and the melting snow left puddles that created a splash when the buggy rode through them. But Kate's mind was on Jonah tensely sitting next to her.

*He's the one who bought these tickets. Why is he so stiff? He hasn't noticed that I'm wearing the barrette he gave me for Christmas. Oh, Lord, help me understand.*

In the small theater, Jonah sat on the aisle seat and placed his arm on the rest next to Kate. Inconspicuously, his large finger wrapped around her smaller finger. His arm tensed then relaxed but only a little.

*He is trying, and that's all that matters . . . right?* Kate tried to convince herself.

The lights dimmed, and the music started. Kate nudged Jonah and whispered about the costumes or scenery. He nodded, keeping his eyes closed.

"Look," Kate directed with a giggle.

Jonah opened his eyes quickly, smiled weakly and nodded. "Nice."

Kate turned back to the stage, a little frustrated. *He can't enjoy this with his eyes closed.*

At intermission, Ben offered to take the ladies into the salon for a refreshment.

Jonah nodded and moved his legs so they could pass. He stayed in his seat, placing his head in his hands and taking a couple of deep breaths.

The salon teemed with people. Kate asked for a glass of wine and then changed her mind, "I should get something else. Do you have any tea?"

The waiter poured a cup of tea and offered a few sugar lumps. Kate took the cup and saucer to where Erin and Ben stood. They shared small talk about the opera for a few minutes until the new electric lights flickered, informing everyone that intermission was almost over. Kate returned her teacup and hurried to her seat.

Back inside, for the next act, Jonah kept his eyes closed, jerking slightly when the stage crew crashed large symbols together, imitating the sound of thunder.

*Is Erin right? Is he thinking of me not himself? He looks miserable.*

The opera ended, and Jonah rushed out the door. In the buggy, he sat next to Kate, eyes shut tight, appearing overwhelmed.

Softly, in Jonah's ear, Kate asked, "Why did you do this if you hate it so much? I already had some things planned for us."

Eyes closed, head leaning back on the seat, he whispered, "Your smile." Then, he started rubbing his back against the seat trying to scratch an itch.

*Really? He really hates social outings. It not just when he has too much going on. He just doesn't like them at all. But he still set this one up, and he did it for me.*

"Take your jacket off." she quietly instructed.

Jonah gave her a look of uncertainty.

Kate smiled and gently tugged at it. He took his jacket off with a questioning brow furrow. Kate placed her hands on his back, encouraging him to lean forward. Then, she began to scratch his back with her long nails.

A pleased moan escaped him. Jonah hunched over more, melting into a ball.

Erin looked back, asking, "What are you two doing back there?"

Jonah groaned, "Anything she wants. She could rule the world right now."

Meeting Kate's eyes, Erin smiled her approval. Kate was thinking of him, not herself. She was thinking about what she could do for the man she loved, receiving nothing in return.

### FRIDAY, APRIL 17

Jonah walked up and down the counter at the jeweler's shop. It was mid-April, and he was looking for something nice for Kate. Her birthday was next week. He had made a carving for her, but he wanted something pretty, something she could wear. Nothing seemed good enough. She had earbobs, bracelets, and necklaces. There had to be something here for her.

*Lord, you know I've been praying about giving her a ring but I'm not sure about the timing. When do You want me to ask her? Should I just give her something else, like a hairbrush set?*

Then he spotted it. It was perfect. A gold ring, with a ruby surrounded by diamonds in the shape of a heart. Jonah gulped as he realized it was an engagement ring.

The jeweler, Mr. Jenkins, offered to bring it out so he could get a better look. The closer look made Jonah more aware of how much Kate would love it. His heart beat hard, knowing what the ring meant. *It must be time! Thank You, God for this perfect ring.*

"Could you hold it for me? I need to go to the bank and . . . talk to someone." Jonah shoved his trembling hands deep in his pockets.

"Yes, but tomorrow morning it goes back in the case for anyone," Mr. Jenkins warned.

Jonah watched the jeweler put the ring in a bag with his name on it. He knew the trip to the bank would be easy. He had the money set aside. It may pinch for a bit, but it was worth it. The trip to the courthouse, where the mayor's office was located, would be the hard part.

*Walk fast. Don't give yourself a chance to put it off. I know she'll say yes. I think Mayor Goodwin will too. But there is still something unnerving about asking this question.*

The courthouse attendant let Jonah in Mayor Goodwin's office. Mayor Goodwin sat behind his desk, shuffling through some papers. Jonah cleared his throat and the mayor looked up.

"Problem?"

"No." Jonah took several deep breaths. "It's been a respectable amount of time."

Mayor sat back with a half grin. "And?"

Jonah closed his eyes and asked, "Can I have Kate's hand in marriage?"

The silence was deafening. Jonah stood with his eyes closed, waiting for an answer. The wait seemed forever. Jonah peeked with one eye, to see what the mayor was doing. He sat at his desk with folded hands, watching Jonah.

"Ask me again with your eyes open, young man."

Another deep breath, both eyes opened, respecting Mayor Goodwin, he asked, "Can I please have Kate's hand in marriage? I love her. I want to spend the rest of my life making her smile."

The mayor broadly grinned. "When I asked you to let her come help you, I had hoped for some growing up in a few days. The match is more than I ever imagined or hoped for. Yes, you can have her hand and her heart."

Jonah beamed. "I got the perfect ring waiting." He ran out the door and back to the jewelers.

He had lots of planning ahead, he wanted things to be perfect; she deserved nothing less.

Later that evening, Jonah drove the team to Kate's house. He had been planning the proposal all day. *I gotta tell the fellas I'm cutting the evening short. I'll have to tell them why, but they will understand. I just gotta keep Kate in the dark for now.*

At the Goodwins' house, Kate met him on the porch. She scurried to the wagon inhaling the fresh spring air.

Kate tossed the lap blanket back. "It's such a beautiful evening. I just had to wait outside and smell the fresh air and flowers."

She pulled herself up to the seat bench and found a red rose next to a carving of a cat.

"Jonah, how beautiful!" She sighed, smiling her love and appreciation.

Sitting down, she admired the cat carving. The feline was curled in a ball. On its back was engraved, "I love you, Katie Cat."

"Jonah, this is the most wonderful thing!" she exclaimed, as she smelled the flower.

"Happy birthday. I know it's early but just in case I forget or I'm busy with work." He pointed to the words. "And just in case I forget to tell you."

She snuggled up closer to him. "Thank you. I love you, too. Oh, and Mother wants to have you over for dinner for my birthday. Can I tell her yes?"

"Of course." He smiled to himself. *I know you'll say yes so there will be a lot to talk about then. But still . . . this is nerve wracking.*

The Club met at Ben and Erin's place that night. Erin loaded the table with a few new dishes she was trying out. The men groaned their appreciation for the good food, and they talked about current political events. Soon, the dishes were gathered and washed, and then Kate and Erin went to the parlor, talking and making plans for Easter at the church.

After the verse was quoted, Jared was shuffling cards, and Jonah said quietly, almost in a whisper, "I'm gonna have to call it early tonight."

The fellas looked at him, puzzled. Jonah's smile grew so large his cheeks hurt just a bit. He put his finger to his lips and pulled out the ring.

Smiles, pats on the back, and nods told him they all agreed with his plans. Paul gave a grin and a slight nod to Jonah, expressing his approval.

Jonah had a hard time keeping his mind on the game. He heard Kate in the other room and imagined his plans for later.

When the clock struck eight, he said, "I'm out." He walked into the parlor and asked Kate if she was ready to leave.

Kate looked at the clock in surprise. "That was a fast game."

"Not my night for cards."

Jonah led her to the buggy, trying hard to control the trembles. As she began to climb in the buggy, Erin was heard squealing with delight inside the house.

Baffled, Kate looked at Jonah. "What's that about?"

"Who knows," Jonah fibbed. He hurried over to his seat, rushing the horses out before anything else gave away his plans.

At the Goodwins', Jonah tethered the team and led Kate to a bench in the garden. She shot Jonah a questioning look but followed him without complaint.

He sat Kate on a stone bench under a blossoming almond tree. Everything was perfect. A cool spring evening set the mood with a soft breeze allowing the sweet scent of wildflowers and blossoms to drift in the air. Crickets chirped a quiet serenade. A bright moonlight filtered through the night sky.

And Kate . . . she was as beautiful as always. Her hair was rolled in a soft chignon, fastened with the barrette he had given her at Christmas. A light azure shawl draped over her shoulders highlighting her deep blue eyes.

Jonah knelt on one knee. Kate's trembling hands flew to her mouth, and her eyes widened.

"Katie Cat, I love you so much. Would you please make me the happiest man alive and marry me?" He held the ring out to her.

She nodded, speechless, offering her left hand. He placed the ring on her finger and kissed it.

Kate pulled him up to the bench, kissing him deeply. The kiss lingered, becoming more passionate, hinting of the intimacy that would come after the wedding.

A tap at the window told them it was time to part. Jonah walked Kate into the house, holding her hand.

With one look at the ring, Mrs. Goodwin began crying. Then she hugged anyone in reach, including the house help. "Oh, my baby! I have been saving articles and such. We will have a perfect wedding."

Kate leaned against Jonah's shoulder. "Mother. Please. Give me a chance. And remember, Jonah likes small groups. We can have a small, beautiful wedding. But a small one."

Her mother tapped her finger on her chin. "We shall see."

ONE WEEK LATER
BEN AND ERIN'S HOUSE

Showing her ring to everyone at the Club, Kate beamed, and recounted the proposal.

A blush flamed Jonah's cheeks. *I don't like attention, but this is good attention, I think.*

"He said all that?" Erin asked at the dinner table. The rest of the Club sat in amused disbelief that Jonah had offered such an eloquent proposal.

Jonah's blush deepened, glowing through his beard. "I wrote it down and practiced all day," he admitted bashfully.

Kate gave him a quick kiss on his rosy cheek. "It was wonderful." Then she turned to Erin. "We have some work to do. Mother is already making plans." Dejectedly she added, "It would be nice if I were included."

Erin laughed. "I guess you and your mother are not seeing eye to eye? Is she just taking over like she often does? We used to laugh about that as children."

"It's not so funny now. Maybe we can get ahead of her, or maybe you can help me convince her that we don't need to have the wedding in Paris."

"Paris? Why Paris?" Erin cleared the table.

"Because it is the most romantic city in the world. Isn't that a good enough reason?" Kate rolled her head in frustration. "At least that is what Mother keeps saying."

The women left to the parlor and Paul started shuffling cards.

Jonah watched his future wife leave the room and then sank into his chair. "She's the best thing that ever happened to me. But there are still some things to work out."

Ben asked, "Like what? It may not be as bad as you think."

"I had no idea that houses were so important to women. We were talking about the wedding, and I mentioned how nice it would be for Mama to have company and help with the housework. Kate was furious. She expects us to get our own house. Why should we? The place is big enough for the three of us. If we found our own place, Mama would have to take care of that big house by herself, and she's beginning to struggle with the work." Jonah sighed and looked around the table. "What am I gonna do?"

"Have you talked to your mother?" Jared asked. "You are assuming a lot on her part. She may not want to live with you and a new wife."

Jonah thought about Jared's idea. "I could talk to her, but what would Mama do if she didn't live at home?"

From the parlor Erin called, "Talk to her and find out. There's more to that woman than you give credit."

Jonah huffed a small laugh. The sound from the kitchen to the parlor carried easily, making private kitchen conversation almost impossible.

"I will, tonight." Then he added, "I promise."

Saturday, June 20
Jonah and Kate's wedding

Jonah paced Jared's office with the rest of the Club, milling around, waiting for the ceremony to start. The Bachelor's Club was shrinking—or was it growing? It was now becoming three bachelors, plus two husbands and two women.

"Don't forget Mama," Jonah nervously reminded his friends.

Ben patted his shoulder. "Don't worry. We will help her move to Billington with her sister while you are on your honeymoon. No need to worry about her."

"I didn't know she wanted to move there. I guess she has wanted it for a while now but didn't want me living on my own. Now that I've got Kate, Mama wants to move. Who knew?"

Ben raised one eyebrow. "Where's your mama staying tonight?"

"She has a bag packed and will leave with Auntie after dinner tonight. She will come back Monday to help you all get her things moved. She said she wanted to start her new life as soon as she can." Jonah looked around with tears welling up. "Her new life, in Billington, without Papa. I wish Papa were here."

"I know how you feel. Knowing my parents would never see Erin and me get married was hard. But you've got your mama," Ben empathized.

Together, in Jared's office, the men prayed, praising God for the blessings He provided.

Entering the sanctuary, Jonah was overwhelmed with emotion. *Why would God give me such an amazing woman? I've learned so much about love and God's grace. I know I have more to learn with Kate at my side. But with God and Kate's love, many of my fears have been conquered—or at least they're getting conquered. Thank You, God.*

The doors in the back opened, and he saw the most beautiful sight he had ever seen—Kate, dressed in white, on her father's arm, carrying a bouquet of blue lilies, looking at *him*, walking to *him*.

Tears struggled as they said their vows. Jared gave Jonah the privilege to kiss his bride. Slowly, Jonah lifted the veil. Tears sparkled in Kate's eyes, as Jonah softly kissed the lips of his *wife*. Jared introduced Mr. and Mrs. Jonah Layton and the crowd cheered.

Mayor Goodwin had spared no expense on his daughter's special day. Tables were lined with white table linens. China plates, crystal goblets, and silver utensils graced each setting. Candlelight flickered from candelabras throughout the hall.

Several courses were prepared for dinner. Salad, veal, rice, and vegetables were served before the cake was cut.

Jonah held Kate's hand as they sliced the first piece of cake. He gently fed it to her, thinking of the tradition. He knew it symbolized his promise to keep her fed and taken care of. The pressure of such a gesture and the eyes watching him made him want to run and hide. But he was next to Kate, it was for her, and he loved her more than he could have ever imagined.

The band played a soft waltz for Jonah and Kate's first dance as husband and wife. A champagne toast was given. Jonah used his water glass to toast and celebrate.

The reception soon ended, and Jonah drove the team back to the house. He remembered driving Erin and Ben home the night of their wedding, but tonight was just for him and Kate. No one else was invited. He carried her over the threshold, and then excused himself to take care of the team. Kate smiled and said she had some things to take care of herself.

Jonah came back in after tending the team and called for Kate. "Katie, where are you?" He looked around, trying to find his wife.

"I'm here," her voice floated down the stairs.

Jonah raced up to his bedroom. He opened the door to find the room empty. Fond memories of childhood filled his head. Toy trains and horses he had carved as a lad were scattered on shelves. The bed he had slept in and now was too long for, sat empty in one corner.

*I never did get that new bed. I can barely fit in there, how will we?*

"Kate?" he called again, wondering where she was.

"In here." Her voice drifted down the hall.

He stepped out and glanced around. The door to his parents' room was opened a crack, and it sounded like she was in there.

*Why's she in Mama's room?*

He pushed the door open to find Kate standing next to the bed in a gossamer gown. All thoughts left his mind as he relished the sight. In two steps, he was holding Kate in his arms.

The room that was once his parents' now became theirs. In front of friends and family, they had accepted the responsibilities of husband and wife. Tonight, alone, they would seal that commitment.

CHAPTER 11

# A New Beginning

FRIDAY, JULY 3

THE LAYTON HOUSE

*This is the last thank you note. I need to mail them off tomorrow. . . . no Monday. Tomorrow is Independence Day. The Club will be here soon. My first time hosting dinner.*

Kate tucked the note into the envelope and sealed it.

"Katie! Where are my clothes? I went to lay out my night shirt and can't find it." Jonah stomped down the stairs. "Kate?"

"Here. Let me show you." Kate stacked the pile of thank you notes on the corner of the desk and followed Jonah up the stairs.

His stomps softened slightly, leading Kate to his childhood room. "Umm, Katie, my things are supposed to be in here."

Kate kept walking to the master bedroom, shaking her head.

"No, dear. In here." She held the door open to the large bedroom. "I noticed you slept in here but went in there to dress. I moved all your things in here."

Jonah looked back into his old bedroom. "But . . ."

"Your Papa's things are already in the attic. Mama told me she will get them the next time she comes for a visit." She wrapped her arms around Jonah. "You are man of the house now. You can make this our room. My things are already in here."

"I'm trying. I see the changes around the house, and I try to accept them. It is your house now not Mama's. Sometimes I forget you need to make it yours." His arms encircled her. "I never thought I would like to be captured. But I love being captured in your arms." He bent down and tenderly kissed his wife.

A loud knock interrupted their embrace.

Kate dashed down the stairs. "I think that is Erin!"

Erin and Ben knocked again and peeked in slowly. "Can we come in?"

"Of course." Jonah took the basket from Erin. "We knew you were coming, so we were prepared."

Ben shrugged with a light chuckle. "Nice to have another married man that understands such things."

Kate looked in the basket. "What did you bring? And thank you for your help. I am still arranging the house and can't spend much time learning to cook."

"Well, I went to the bakery. I got some bread and a berry pie. I am still learning to make those. At home, I made a summer salad. What smells so good?"

Kate opened the oven. "I am getting pretty accomplished with baking fish. As soon as we were back, Jonah went fishing. There is enough for everyone to have several fillets. I also made some rice and cauliflower."

Another knock sounded on the front door. "Can I come in?" Corbin cracked the door. "This is the same house, but somehow it feels different."

"Get in here. You are letting flies in. I need to get a netting for the windows and door." Jonah pulled out a chair for Kate, and then sat next to her.

Ben followed, offering Erin a seat. "Things are different, but good."

Next, Paul and Jared knocked on the door. "Are you ready for—"

"Yes!" Jonah laughed. "I've been smelling that fish for some time now. Get in here so we can all eat!"

Paul and Jared joined the group at the table. After prayer, fillets were passed around, and the men helped themselves to the other dishes. Talk about tomorrow's Independence Day festivities filled the air.

When dinner ended, Kate and Erin washed the dishes, while the men pulled out cards and quoted last week's verse.

"Let's go in the parlor and start planning some fall fun. After the celebration tomorrow, I don't know what we will do," Erin prodded.

Kate joined her in the parlor and nestled into a rocking chair. "Now that it is just us and we are both married, I can ask. Any hints of a baby?"

Erin frowned. "I talked to Nurse Meadows. She said to give it some more time. If there is no sign in a few months, I can talk to Doc and see what he thinks."

Gasping, Kate covered her mouth. "Doctor Bells? You could talk to a man about . . . that?"

"I don't know," Erin shrugged and looked away, trying to hide the crimson on her cheeks. "Right now, I am trying to busy myself with things, like the rentals and maybe a fall festivity."

"Well, then, let's talk. Who should—" A knock interrupted Kate.

"Now who could that be at this time of night?" Kate wondered while she answered the door.

A young man, holding a telegram waited. "For Pastor Morris. Is he here?"

Kate's smile dropped. "Yes. I can give it to him." She signed her name on the clipboard. *He looks serious. Who would send a telegram this late at night? And usually it would go to his house and get pushed under the door. It must be bad news to be delivered here.*

Kate took the telegram into the kitchen. Erin followed quietly.

Holding out the telegram, Kate called Jared's attention. "Jared, this is for you."

The laughter in the room died. Jared's grin dipped to a straight line as he took the telegram. He opened it with shaky hands and read silently.

He dropped it on the table. "My family . . . accident . . . hospital . . . Ben cover for me Sunday. I don't know how long I will be gone." Jared rushed out, leaving the telegram.

Ben picked it up. "It says there has been an accident. His parents and sister are in the hospital. Not sure if they will survive the night."

He held out his hands. "We need to pray—and right now."

Ben led the group in prayer. Everyone sat at the table with grim faces. The cards were carelessly scattered around. Erin softly cried.

Kate rubbed her face in her hands. *Lord, he needs You. Please wrap Your love around him. Carry him with Your love.*

# Discussion Questions

1. Kate is an extrovert and Jonah is an introvert. What are you? How do you feel about the opposite personality?

2. Kate wanted Jonah to change for her. Have you ever tried to change someone? Has someone ever tried to change you? What problems were created?

3. Jonah was trying to be more sociable, but he had trouble. Have you ever tried to make changes in yourself? Was there a difference with, or without, God?

4. Jonah and Kate began to think of the other person, and that is when things got better for them. What do you do for someone you love? How do you demonstrate 1 Corinthians 13? Is that chapter only applicable for romantic love? Why or why not?

www.ingramcontent.com/pod-product-compliance
Lightning Source LLC
Chambersburg PA
CBHW050901180626
46814CB00007B/2842